Death on The River Wear

Vicky Peplow

For you Dad. You always saw the best in me. I love you and miss you.

Lorie you are my world

Acknowledgements

First I would like to thank my partner, Lorie Foltz for her support and being there for me. You are my world, and I couldn't imagine life without you in it.

A special thanks goes out to Shani Struthers, Sarah England, and Samantha Talarico, for all of you guidance in the preparation of this book. Also to Mick Naisbitt for the use of your amazing pictures which have been used. A massive thank you to Simon Leonard for first edits and Samantha Talarico for second edits. Thank you also goes out to the amazing, and unappreciated midwives, doctors, scrub nurses, and the maternity support workers (or HCA's when I was there) at the RVI in Newcastle upon Tyne. I had the pleasure of working five amazing years with them and loved every minute.

Last but not least, thank you to Ryhope and Sunderland for being an amazing place to grow up in, and for spurring my imagination.

Prologue

Tyne and Wear. Nothing big usually happens in this part of the world. We have our thieves, our burglars, our murderers and rapists, but nobody ever expected to have a serial killer living, working and sleeping amongst them. Nobody ever thought that all the murders that were happening were linked, or that the same person was responsible until a detective from America came and realized that the disposal site was spread along the River Wear in Sunderland.

In London, it had been a busy day at work for Tracey and all she wanted to do now was get home and put her feet up with a glass of wine. She had received a text from her son, Grayson, letting her know he was coming over for tea that night and asking what was on the menu. She'd texted him back to say they were getting a take away instead.

The roads were pretty busy tonight but then, they always were in England's busy capital city and that made her think of how quiet the roads were back home in Ryhope at this time of night. As always, thinking of home, she felt a little nostalgic, but she also thought of the horror she'd gone through and it made her shiver a little.

Grayson was texting again and, although driving, she was busy texting back, taking her eyes off the road ahead when she suddenly saw the full beam of a car heading straight towards her; a car with no intentions of stopping. As she turned her car to the right in order to avoid him, she felt herself being spun around in the car like a washing machine until finally, the car crashed to a halt.

Tracey knew she was seriously hurt but because of shock, not to what extent. A small part of her brain, the rational part, immediately tried to assess. She was numb from her chest down and it was getting harder to hold on to consciousness. What if she didn't survive this? If she didn't get to see her husband and son again? Panic cut through the numbness and then she remembered she still had her phone in her hand. Desperation spurring her on, she brought her other hand over and pressed Grayson's number again.

Grayson saw that his mam was trying to call him but he was in the middle of his rounds, trying to get finished early so he could go and see his parents for that takeaway. He couldn't answer the phone so he sent it to voicemail.

When Grayson failed to answer, it made Tracey panic further. She didn't have any strength left to try and call anyone else. A voicemail would have to do, so she left a message for Grayson. "Hi son, it's Mam. There's been an accident and I need you to call Dad. Please don't worry and I'll see you soon. I love….."

Chapter 1

"Tickets please," the conductor shouted. "All train tickets from London to Sunderland please have out ready to be seen, Thank you."

Grayson Taylor Shaw rummaged in his pocket trying to find the ever-elusive piece of paper that constituted a ticket. It wasn't in the first pocket he searched, or the second, thankfully he found it, however, in his left trouser pocket, nestling there with a tissue and a ticket from an older journey.

The conductor waited with surprising patience. "Where will you be getting off?" he asked.

"Sunderland."

"Okay, sir, thank you. It all looks to be in order. Have a great day. Enjoy your time in Sunderland."

"Oh I will, thank you."

He certainly intended to enjoy himself, more than that jolly little conductor could ever imagine. At the thought of it, Grayson started chuckling to himself. A respected surgeon in London, he was very good with his hands and that came in handy for his occupation. No one knew that he'd applied for another job in Newcastle upon Tyne, but he had reasons, personal reasons, why he wanted to be in the North-East of England. Of course, he'd get this new job. If anything he was overqualified just to be an orthopaedic surgeon, but he wanted to learn the ropes and the area before chasing for anything bigger.

Settling back into his seat, he took in the countryside as it whizzed past him. He'd never been outside of London in his whole life so this was definitely out of the box for him. He had to find out more about his mam's family, though, as this is where she had come from, his mam who'd recently died in a car accident. Nobody, not even Grayson's dad, knew much about Tracey's background.

He tried to relax, shutting his eyes, the conversation he'd had with his dad starting to replay in his head.

"How can you not know anything about my mam, your wife, before you married her?" he remembered asking, aghast.

Grayson's dad, Patrick, had turned at that, walking over to the counter to pour himself a scotch, drinking it in one go before facing Grayson again.

"Son, your mam didn't like talking about her past before she came to London and I loved her and still love her so much that as far as we were concerned, our lives started when we found each other, when we decided to get married and start a family."

At this point Grayson had been feeling a whole host of mixed emotions: sorrow, happiness, resentment and, of course, anger, which he was finding hard to control.

"Does she have any sisters or brothers? Do I have any aunties or uncles and cousins?"

"She did mention she had two sisters and a brother, but she never mentioned anything about them having had any children. Son, it was all such a long time ago."

Feeling the anger rising again he finally asked; "Do they even know I exist?"

Hanging his head, Patrick had answered, "I don't know son, probably not."

After this Grayson had picked up his jacket and stormed out of his dad's house to go and cool off.

Grayson felt bad about speaking to his dad the way he had, but he needed answers and he needed them now. The only way he could figure out how to find them was to pack up everything in his life and move to the area where his mam was from. Maybe he would like it there, maybe he would stay on.

Because his eyes were closed, he never noticed a young lady a few seats down, who was facing his way and smiling at him.

When he finally opened his eyes, he spotted her and smiled back, which caused her to start giggling with the friend she was sitting with. Grayson was a handsome guy, so why not have a little fun while on a long train journey? With confidence, he rose to go and take the empty seat opposite them, introducing himself; their blushes at his bold actions amusing him. Their names were Julie and Karen; they told him where they worked, where they were going to, where they were staying and last but not least, their phone numbers.

Julie then took the reins. "Maybe we can meet up with you at some point while we're in Newcastle?"

"Yeah sure," replied Grayson, "That sounds like a great idea."

As the train stopped, Karen stood up. "Until then," she said, "We'll definitely be giving you a call."

"I look forward to it, ladies."

Twenty minutes later, the train pulled into Sunderland station and by now Grayson was hungry. He got off the train and hauled his case up the stairs to exit. Friday nights in Sunderland seemed to be busy as what greeted him when he stepped onto the streets were a host of people, all dressed up, seemingly heading to a pub at the end of the street called Sinatra's. There was a lot of noise coming from the pub and he could hear someone trying to sing "My Way" by the pub's namesake, Frank Sinatra, but that's where the similarity ended. Instead of pleasant on the ears, it sounded like a strangled cat was performing it. Nonetheless, Grayson smiled. He wasn't too tired so may come back out a little later and check the pub out, have a couple of drinks.

Just as Grayson thought this his stomach rumbled and he remembered he was hungry. There was a Burger King closer than the pub so he went there and ordered himself a double whopper with fries and a drink then sat down and people watched as he ate his food. Next, he'd have to find out where his flat was, then find a taxi or walk depending on the distance which he could figure out on his phone. He could grab a quick shower, freshen up then decide what he was going to do next.

According to Google Maps, his flat was only a five-minute walk away. Quickly finishing his meal, he walked the distance, and sure enough, five minutes later, he was standing outside his flat. He wasn't the only one: so was another guy, dangling a set of keys, the landlord perhaps?

"Are you, Grayson?" the guy said.

"Yeah, I'm Grayson."

"Ah'reet good, I'm Stephen and here's ya keys for the flat. The rent is due at the end of each month. Put it in an envelope, place it on the sideboard in the living room, and I'll pick it up. Here's a card with my number on; if ya need anything, give me a call and I'll see what I can dee for ya."

Grayson looked at the card and then smiled at Stephen. "That's great. Thank you, Stephen, but I'm sure I'll be okay, and I will contact you if I need anything."

Grayson noticed that Stephen was all dressed up and was itching to get away.

"Nee bother mate, have a good night and I'll see ya around maybe. Okay, I'm gannin out the neet so I've gotta go."

"Okay, you go and have a good night," Grayson replied.

As he wandered off, Stephen's phone began to ring, the theme from Star Wars blasting out before he answered it. "Al'reet I'm coming, dinnit get ya knickers in a twist. I'm on my way now; I just had to drop a set of keys off for a new tenant who's just arrived. I'll be there in ten minutes" Hanging up, he turned back to Grayson. "See ya around, mate. Hope everything is okay for ya, bye," and then he was gone before Grayson could reply goodbye.

Grayson entered his new abode. In the hallway, he placed his bag on the floor and looked around. He was happy with what he saw. He made sure he picked a sparsely furnished flat so that he wouldn't have to go looking for furniture but he was sure he'd probably pick a few pieces up anyway just to put his own stamp on the place and make it more homely. He put his bag down and looked around to see what it looked like, and he was very happy with what he saw. This was definitely going to be his bachelor pad and he was going to be very happy here. He decided over the next couple of days he would go and look around the area and see what was to offer in Sunderland, check out the stores and get some shopping in as everything was empty. Right now, though, he just wanted to freshen up and decide if he was going to go out for a little, as it was still pretty early.

Half an hour later, feeling much fresher, he decided to do just that. He'd check out Sinatra's as at least it looked lively there

Shrugging on a pair of jeans, a shirt and a pair of black shoes, he also splashed on some aftershave which stung a little after just shaving off his five o'clock shadow, combed his hair back and put his watch on. It was only nine-thirty p.m. so things looked good for a good night out. Checking himself in the mirror just before he left, he thought to himself *"let's see what tonight brings, hopefully, I'll be lucky with the ladies"* and then he walked out the door and made his way towards the pub.

Chapter 2

"11-19 what is your current location at this time?"

PC Natalie Roberts really wanted to say, "At this moment in time, I'm sitting outside Gregg's eating a sausage roll and drinking a coffee" but decided against it. Instead, she replied, "11-19 currently waiting for an assignment."

PC Roberts wasn't having a good day and her rookie partner had just let a suspect get away from them just outside of Barclays Bank, which had put her in a really bad mood.

She'd been in the Northumbria Police Force for ten years and was due a promotion, looking to move into the Criminal Investigations Department (CID), but she'd already been looked over for a guy who had been in the force far less time than her and that had really pissed her off. She had a good arrest rate and had commendations for her work from previous assignments. Surely they couldn't pass her over the next time? Natalie was thirty-five years old and born and bred in Sunderland so she knew the streets and the area like the back of her hand. All she could do was breathe deeply and take each day as it came as the time would surely come when she could prove herself a great cop, willing to do anything and everything to get the job done and protect the city she loved.

"11-19 please respond to a possible theft in The Bridges Shopping Center. Security guards are currently watching two white teenage males in HMV music store getting ready to steal DVD's, headphones, and other accessories, and they'd like backup from us."

"11-19 responding to The Bridges Shopping Center with 29-31," Natalie replied.

"10-4, 11-19, and please try not to lose these teenagers if it is a theft."

Seeing red at that response, Natalie turned to her colleague. "Did you hear what she just said, Edwards? DO NOT LOSE them this time."

Peter Edwards, a rookie cop, was only twenty years old and had only been on the police force for six months. Natalie was his first partner in the field and he'd already made a bad impression with her by losing the thief that had stolen a woman's handbag as she was leaving the bank. In fairness, he'd given chase to catch the thief but lost him when he had ran into the very same shopping centre they were about to head to now.

He had been so apologetic. "I'm sorry, Officer Roberts, I really don't know where the guy went." he had said. "One minute he was right in front of me and the next he was gone. I really thought I had him as soon as I got in Bridges."

Natalie had looked at Edwards with squinted eyes. "Okay, well don't let it happen again and not on my watch as I'm the one who gets it in the neck with you being a rookie. It goes on my record, not yours."

Edwards' cheeks had turned red. "Yeah, sorry about that and no, I won't let it happen again"

Feeling sorry for him as well as frustrated, she'd relented. "Look, stop with all this Roberts stuff. Only call me that in official capacity, any other times just call me Natalie or Nat. You're making me feel old calling me by my surname all the time."

Edwards brought his head up and smiled at Natalie, "Then please feel free to call me Peter."

"Nah, rookie suits you better." She'd turned her head as she said it so Peter wouldn't catch her smile. She knew full well they couldn't catch every bad guy or girl out there but she was sure as hell going to try.

They parked their patrol car then walked the rest of the way to Bridges where they met two security guards who didn't exactly look happy to see them. They were both tall, one with a fully- grown beard, the other clean shaven with dark hair parted to the side. Both guys towered over Natalie, but Peter, at six foot, at least matched them in height.

"11-19 and 29-31 on the scene at The Bridges Shopping Center," Natalie informed control. Control responded "10-4, 11-19."

"You took ya bloody time to get 'ere, didn't ya?" the bald one said.

"You called for backup, guys," Natalie ignored the scathing sarcasm in his voice. "What's the situation regarding the suspected thieves in HMV?"

"They've already gotten away because you took your bloody time. Never send a lass and a boy to do a bloke's job."

"Hey! This lass and boy were coming to help you lads do your job. You're two big strapping lads and yet you let those youngsters get away from you. What's the point of employing you if ya can't even do ya job? Idiots!" Natalie was starting to get pissed off with the security guards.

Peter clearly noticed her losing her cool and so took over. Taking out his notebook, he wrote down the description of the two escapees. One had short hair, the other shoulder length. The short-haired teen was wearing a black Adidas tracksuit with a pair of white trainers, and the long-haired teen was wearing a blue Nike tracksuit top, blue jeans and a pair of Nike trainers. Peter thanked the security guards and told them that's all they needed but to keep a lookout in case the teens came back. Both guards turned and walked back into the shopping centre. Peter then called in to control to give them the descriptions so other officers in the area could be on the lookout for them. He then told control they were both clear and waiting for their next job.

Natalie had regained her composure. "Thanks for taking over there, rookie. People like that really know how to piss me off and make my blood boil."

"It's okay, I understand. People like that give us a bad name and I'm your partner, so it was my job to help out and not just stand there like a mannequin."

This made Natalie laugh and even more when Peter had called himself a mannequin. Just thinking of it made her laugh even more. Back in the patrol car she suggested they go and grab a coffee.

"Sounds good to me," Peter replied, looking really quite chuffed that he'd been able to amuse her.

With him gone to get the coffees, Natalie started thinking about what she had planned for the weekend. She was going to see her mother on Saturday morning and go into town with her for a little while, before heading home. Saturday afternoon was also going to be busy as she was going to go and watch the football match at the Stadium of Light with her partner Lauren, then probably go out for drinks afterwards. Sunday was her day to relax and maybe go and see some other family members but that depended on if she could be bothered to even leave her apartment. Decisions, decisions, maybe even a day in bed could be on the cards and a marathon of Grey's Anatomy on Netflix.

"Earth to Mars, come in Mars."

Peter had come back from getting the coffees and looked in need of a helping hand in opening the car doors. She got out of the car and took her coffee from him as well as a chocolate éclair.

"Oh, I'm sorry. I must have been in my own little world there thinking about what I was gonna do this weekend."

"Hey, what's this?" she said, looking at it. "I thought you were just getting coffees?"

Peter shrugged. "Sorry, I couldn't resist."

Natalie smiled. "The American cops have doughnuts and we have éclairs, eh? Are you trying to get me fat or summit?"

"Nah, I just thought it'd be a nice treat while we wait for our next job, that's all."

"It's okay, rookie, I'm just messing with ya and thank you it's very thoughtful, I'll enjoy it. You did get me a coffee with milk and plenty of sugar, right?"

"I sure did and you are very welcome. It's your turn next time though. Cost me an arm and a leg for these."

"Yeah, yeah, I'll get the next ones."

Natalie and Peter were in the patrol car for about two hours before anything came through from control. Most of the time, they people watched, honking their horn at a group of kids harassing an old lady at a bus stop, causing them to take flight.

Growing extremely bored, the police radio suddenly roared into action.

"11-19 and 29-31 respond to the south side of the Queen Alexandra Bridge. Body found of a young white female near water's edge by a couple walking. Detectives informed and coroner. Please corner off area until more details are given at the scene."

The hairs on Natalie's arms stood on end. These were the calls she hated, but she also knew that this was the time to prove herself worthy of the promotion she'd previously applied for.

"11-19 and 29-31 responding to the scene," she said. "Please be advised to send back up in case the suspect is still in the area and also to help control traffic if need be."

"10-4, 11-19, other cars also responding."

"10-4 control."

This was going to be the rookie's first murder scene. Hopefully, the coffee and eclair he'd just consumed weren't going to make a second appearance because, by the sounds of it, this wasn't going to be pretty. Then again, what murder scene was? She was starting to have a little faith in Edwards, so hopefully, things wouldn't be too bad for him... unless there was that putrid smell of decay. In the ten years she'd been on the force, Natalie had seen her fair share of murders and the trick she had been learned was to stick Vick's vapour rub in your nostrils to mask the smell. Reaching over to the glove box, she retrieved the small blue jar and handed it to Peter, explaining the tradition.

"Are you ready for your first murder, rookie?" Natalie asked Peter as he hadn't said anything since the report had come over the radio.

"Yes," he nodded. "Unfortunately needs must."

"You'll be okay. The Vicks won't get rid of the smell completely but it'll help. If you feel like you're going to throw up, move away from the crime scene, catch your breath, then come back. Stick with me rookie, and you'll be fine."

"Thanks for the advice, Natalie, I appreciate it."

"No problem. We're nearly there so prepare yourself and do as I say."

Peter gave Natalie a thumbs up and as he didn't want her to know that he was petrified and hoped it didn't show, but Natalie was smart and she probably already knew that he was.

The patrol car came to a stop at the spot where crowds and cars were already starting to build up. Natalie knew she had to get them moving before homicide got on scene. That could be Peter's job; he could clear the traffic and people until back-up came then he could join her. Meanwhile she would get witness statements from the couple who found the body. It may not even be a murder, she reminded herself, but a suicide as people had a thing about jumping off bridges and into the murky water of the Wear below.

When the backup came, she and Peter made their way to the edge of the river to where the body was. What they saw was enough to turn anyone's stomach. This was definitely *not* a suicide and Natalie knew that. Homicide was definitely needed.

Chapter 3

After a couple days of settling into his new surroundings and getting to know the area, Grayson was starting to enjoy himself. He'd bought a few things for his new apartment, and it was starting to feel a little like a home away from home. He did the tourist thing and went around Sunderland city centre to see the attractions such as the City Library, the National Glass Centre, Sunderland Museum and Winter Gardens and checked the Bridges shopping centre.

The pubs in the city he found very entertaining as there was plenty of them, maybe even more so than in London. What he found entertaining in particular were the individuals that came in and mostly fell out of the pubs at all hours of the day and that nobody around even seemed to care.

Grayson still had another couple of weeks before he started work at the Royal Victoria Infirmary in Newcastle which he was essentially looking forward to. A few people that he'd chatted to over a couple of beers informed him the locals called it the RVI and that it had a good reputation. Already he'd checked out his route and how long it would take him to get to work, around forty minutes on foot. Grayson had also picked up through general chatter around him that people from Newcastle called themselves Geordies and people from Sunderland were Mackems and both sets of people hated each other, especially if they played against each other in football. Other areas had nicknames too but a lot of them sounded crazy and he honestly couldn't remember them. Perhaps he'd pick them up in time.

He'd also been told about a shopping centre called the MetroCentre, supposed to be the largest in the UK. That was on his 'to see' list too.

When Grayson got back to Sunderland from Newcastle, it was late. He resolved to have an early night and maybe a takeaway. Food in the North-East of England was diverse from anything down south, but he was getting used to trying new things. He didn't really want to tell people or show that he came from a wealthy background and had money that he'd earned of his own accord, and he didn't need or want any trouble because of it while he was here. He finally plumped for pizza, which he'd pick up en-route back to his flat, plus a couple more bottles of beer from the local corner shop.

When Grayson got home and settled in front of the TV, he switched the news on. There was an update on the body of a young lady that had been found the week before, but still nobody had come forward with a name or details regarding her. They were asking for help from anyone that was in the area around twelve midnight and one a.m. on the day of the murder. A tip line number was now on the screen showing all calls were anonymous and that rewards would be offered for information. Grayson turned the TV over after the report had finished and didn't think any more of it as he worked his way through another slice of pizza from the box, noting that a Fast & Furious film was just about to start - one of his favourites.

The evening passed satisfyingly enough and the next day Grayson woke around eleven a.m., slumped on the couch where he'd been eating pizza, drinking beer and watching Vin Diesel burst out through the back of a fiery plane. Rising, he headed to the bathroom to take a shower and brush his teeth.

Today was going to be the day he'd begin finding out what he could about the place his mam had come from. He knew from the maps on his phone that her place of birth was a few miles south along the coast from Sunderland, and he could either get a bus or taxi to get there, but before that he wanted to do more digging. Grayson still couldn't believe that nobody knew any history surrounding his mother, his father especially. Why hadn't he sought to find out the bare minimum?

Opening up his laptop, he decided he'd also try the ancestry sites. Some of his friends had used these sites before and found out some amazing things about their family members and their past lives. Some had found things about past great, great grandfathers or their twice removed uncle who had served in the army and had died or was wounded during a great war. He almost smiled himself as he remembered other tales he'd been told by friends, that a family member had spent time in prison for either murder, rape, or robbing a bank and the consequence of that was they were hanged or died in prison!

He entered his mother's details and a list of people with the same name as her came up. That was something he had learnt from his dad, that his mam's maiden name was Self. He clicked on the option of Tracey Self and it brought up that she was indeed born in Sunderland. Her parents were Robert and Annie Self and, from the census he'd found, they had, in fact, lived in Ryhope, Sunderland. He continued to look through details to find his mother had, in fact, four sisters and one brother. One of the sisters had died a few years back but the other three were still living and so was her brother. Grayson now knew he had three aunties and an uncle, probably a couple of cousins too.

With the new material that Grayson had just found, he now knew that he had to go to Ryhope to find his family and learn about his mother and meet his other family members. He didn't know why but he was starting to get apprehensive about going and wondered if he should just leave things alone in case he found out something he didn't want to know.

He shut the computer down and decided take a walk and determine what his next step was going to be. It was a nice day so a walk around Mowbray Park would be good to clear his thoughts. Later, Grayson was ready and picked up his belongings; put his earphones in his ears as he was walking out, as he didn't want any outside interference while out walking. While walking he started thinking what if his mother was in danger and had to flee to the south to get away and met his father when she got to London, or if she'd done something and fled to London to get away from the authorities. All different scenarios were flying through his head while walking. He didn't see the couple walking their dog and apologized for nearly walking into them or the car that was coming towards him when he crossed the road and nearly ran him over.

He didn't hear the car horn as his music was playing full blast in his ears. A little Queen was good when walking and it drowned out every noise around him. The guy in the car shouted, "Hey, man, watch where ya gannin! I nearly knocked ya ower there."

Grayson was shocked and didn't realize he was so close. "I'm so sorry, I didn't realize you were as close."

The guy in the car looked at him. "Nee bother mate, just be careful next time will ya or ya gonna get ya self killed," he responded.

He'd now been out for over an hour walking around and his walk had taken him out of Mowbray Park and towards Park Lane Bus Station and back through the city centre towards his flat.

Grayson was going to go out later so when he got home he showered again, had something to eat, and rested for a little in front of the TV. Grayson had become friends with the guys in the flat above, and they'd arranged to meet up a couple of days before to go out for a few drinks, and then maybe go to a club later.

Chapter 4

Peter wanted to ask Natalie some questions but didn't know how to word it and not sound like a complete idiot or rude for asking. He had suspicions but didn't want to assume anything, and he'd rather ask and get the details instead. Peter kept looking at Natalie and, was going to say something but decided against it at the last second.

Natalie knew he was trying to say something, but she figured it wasn't important or he just didn't know how to come out with it. She was going to wait for a moment longer because it was fun for her to watch him squirm a little out of the corner of her eye.

Time had gone past and he'd still not built up the courage to ask his questions. She was starting to get impatient now and wished he would just ask whatever it was he wanted to know. They'd been partners for a while now and they had become friends as well as just colleagues. It came to where Natalie would catch the suspect and Peter would book them in at the police station and he'd finish the paperwork that needed done. She was a hands-on kind of cop, not a paper pusher.

"Rookie, do you have something you wanna say or are you having a seizure or something?" Natalie finally asked as she'd lost patience.

"I do but I don't know how to say it without being rude or coming across in the wrong way."

"Okay, take a minute then just come out with it as we haven't got all day."

"Okay, here it goes. Ya can tell me to mind my own business and stay out of ya personal life but ya seem to mention Lauren a lot when we chat. I was just wondering if she was your girlfriend." Natalie was wondering when this conversation was going to arise and she actually expected it a lot earlier. She changed positions in her seat so she was looking directly at Peter.

"Yes, Lauren is my girlfriend and yes, it is my personal life which I don't care to discuss while I'm at work."

"Ah right okay, I can respect that" Peter continued on, "I figured.

"This made Natalie smirk, "What made you ask that question anyway?"

Peter sat thinking and his character changed and replied. "My younger sister, she was gay and I used to go out with her drinking every now and then." Natalie knew what he was talking about but then she finally realized that Peter had spoken in the past tense.

Natalie wanted to ask what he meant, but she kind of figured it might be something that he didn't want to delve into.

Peter saw that the question was there on the tip of her tongue but she had respect for him not to ask unless he wanted to share. He was okay with it as he'd already grieved for his sister and so had his family.

"You're wondering why I said was and not is, right?" Peter noticed that Natalie was trying to figure it out in her head.

"Yeah, but if you don't want to say, then that's okay." Natalie acknowledged.

"No, no, my little sister Joanne died last year while I was at the Police training academy. She'd lost her fight against stage four last year."

"My deepest condolences, Peter. I'm sure it's been a hard time for you and your family."

"Thank you, she didn't even know she was sick until she'd went to the doctors for a routine checkup and they pressed on her stomach and it was painful. We were very close as there's only a year between us. My mam called me, told me to get home as quickly as possible as she had something to tell me. I was heartbroken when she told me and I thought she was playing a sick prank on me but no, it definitely was no joke. The doctor had given her six months to live but she lived for nine months as she was definitely a little fighter."

Peter looked at Natalie and he could feel his eyes were getting wet and he hoped that Natalie didn't notice. "Can we change the subject to something different as I have something else to ask you, and this may question your beliefs and religion?"

"Yeah, go ahead, shoot. What's the next question?" Natalie asked.

"Do you believe in the paranormal?" Peter asked inquisitively.

"Do you mean in like ghosts and stuff like that or do you mean supernatural like vampires, werewolves etc.?" she inquired.

"Nah, I mean in ghosts and that kinda stuff"

"Ah right okay, yeah I guess I do, but I'd rather say that I'm open-minded about it. I do like watching Ghost Hunters, Ghost Adventures, The Dead Files and Paranormal Lockdown and that sort of thing, but I've never personally heard or seen anything. Why, have you seen or heard something?" she wondered.

"I'm not actually sure. I always feel like my sister is around me; that gives me some comfort and I'd like to think that she is my guardian angel. I always wondered if people that have been, ya know, murdered or have taken their own life or the people that have died in car crashes etc., if they stay grounded here because they have some unfinished business or don't even know that they've died if it was sudden."

Natalie looked at Peter and replied, "Wow! Rookie, that's some deep shit you're talking about there but definitely some interesting questions to think about. Personally, I would like to think we go to a better place when our life here is finished but like you said, what about the people that don't know they are dead."

"Yeah, exactly, but I guess that's one of the questions everybody wants to know."

"Yeah, you're probably right there, rookie."

They were contemplating the conversations they'd just had and didn't even realized how much time had gone past when the radio came to life and they both knew it was time to get back to their day jobs of being cops.

"11-19 please respond to a body found of a young lady at the Hylton Viaduct. An eye-witness who found the victim is still at the scene and will be waiting for your arrival. Homicide and coroner informed and heading to the scene."

"10-4 control, on our way."

"Copy 11-19."

It was Natalie's turn to drive the patrol car so she headed towards the viaduct. She hadn't been here since she was a kid with her friends, but she knew how to get there. Once they got there, it was imperative to protect the evidence, which from what she could tell, was the body; she made sure that nobody was contaminating the evidence in case the suspect that killed her, left any trace evidence they could collect. Today Peter was going to take a statement from the eyewitness and make sure that he got all the details and a number from her in case she needed to be contacted. Natalie found it strange, the scene looked familiar to her, and also the wounds to the young lady seemed identical to the body that had been found at the Alexander Bridge. Homicide came and took over the crime scene and the coroner came to claim the body and take it to the medical examiner's office to find the cause of death.

Peter had finished doing the jobs that he'd been given, and then returned to Natalie. It was time to take the patrol car back to the station and time to go for a couple of drinks and get something to eat as they hadn't eaten for a few hours now and he was starving.

"What you thinking about partner?" he asked Natalie.

"I was just thinking how similar this murder is to the one at Alexander Bridge. Did you see any similarities between them?"

"Now that you mention it, they do seem very similar. Do you think that they are connected or just very similar?"

"I'm not sure but something to maybe check out at some point. Maybe I'm just tired and over-thinking it."

"Sounds good to me. Do you fancy going for a quick pint and something to eat? Give Lauren a call and get her to meet us at Jamieson's. I'll pay for the food as I'm starving and I think a pint would go down well right now."

"Yeah, why not? I'll call Lauren now and get her to meet us there in thirty minutes. If you're paying for the meals, then I'll pay for the drinks."

"Okay, that's a deal." Peter answered.

Natalie hadn't planned on going out for a drink but after that last job, a bottle or two would be nice; she could do with a good meal as they hadn't eaten in a while. Lauren asked if she could meet her rookie partner and now was as good a time as ever, plus it got Lauren out of cooking, but Natalie knew that she was at work early in the morning and that was a perfect excuse to leave a little earlier.

Chapter 5

It was raining outside today but that wasn't going to stop Grayson from checking out Durham City and the Cathedral. Grayson had eventually found himself a car and a nice one at that. A Mercedes C Class C350 eSports Premium which he thought would do him for now. He wasn't planning on using it much but it would come in useful when it came to driving out of town.

It was nearly mid-day by the time he'd showered and got ready before he sat down in front of the television to have breakfast before he left for Durham. The mid-day news was on television and it was talking about a body being found at the Hylton Viaduct and all help was needed to find the suspect in this crime and another crime stoppers number was on the screen and urging people to call with any useful information. Next on the news was about sport and the Sunderland football team and who they were playing this weekend. Grayson liked football and had recently been to a Sunderland game, which they had lost to Liverpool, but the atmosphere of the fans was amazing. His team was Arsenal and they had won their last game and were playing Manchester United this weekend, so he would see if that game would be on television and watch it; if not then he would live stream it on his laptop.

Next week he would start work at the RVI, so he would make sure that he had a good night sleep the night before as he would be up bright and early that day and would be using the metro to get to work as he'd already planned and routed the directions he would take. He was already getting emails from the secretary of what his first week on the job would include and the doctor he would be following and observing until he got his own workload. He also had a meeting with his boss at eleven a.m. that he could not miss. In his first week, he would be on Ward 23, which was an adult trauma orthopaedic ward, and Ward 42 which is a complex Spinal Unit and also the fracture clinic. After this, he would rotate to the Emergency Room and see to any emergency orthopaedic cases that came in and decide if they needed surgery or not.

Now in his car to Durham, he noticed how beautiful the countryside was and that he would have to walk around it someday and see everything up close. It didn't take him long to get to Durham, but he was certain it would've taken longer on the bus. He found a parking spot pretty easily, probably because of it raining and not many people being out and about. The first place he was going to go and look at was the Durham Museum and Heritage Centre. From the website, it said that they had a reconstruction of a Victorian prison cell which would be interesting, and he was interested in seeing what exhibitions they had regarding the local area. After there he was going to check out Durham Castle and the Cathedral, as that was the touristy thing to do. Apparently, there was the fourteenth century

Monks' Dormitory with original best-preserved oak beamed ceilings to see at the Cathedral as well as many other things. After checking these places he would get back in the car and drive to Beamish Museum and see what that had to offer. As far as he knew it was a place where people dressed in old-fashioned clothes and taught you the history of what it was like living in this part of the country in the early 1900's. After Grayson had done all that, he would find somewhere nice to eat and have a good meal before he headed back to his apartment, maybe going to the local pub before settling for the night and watching some television before he went to bed.

By the time he got to his apartment and parked the car, it was six-thirty p.m. so he decided to just go straight to the pub and have a couple of drinks. When he went, he enjoyed sitting with the old timers as they had plenty of stories about the area and when they were in the Navy, Army, or Air Force which Grayson quite liked to hear, and it passed the time away. He hadn't even noticed that he'd had four drinks and three hours had gone past. It was time for him to say goodbye to his old friends and he promised them he would see them again soon as he would like to hear some more of the stories they had to tell.

Grayson had to take his bottles to the bar so they could disregard them into a bottle bin when he realized a young lady at the bar was watching him. He only had four bottles, so he knew he was drunk or imagining it, so he looked back towards her to make sure she was looking at him and she was, so he smiled back. She had blonde hair, blue eyes, was wearing a black dress with black heels, and she had a body to die for. Grayson was too busy looking her up and down to realize that she was talking to him

"Hey, my eyes are up here," she'd said, "not down there. That's for later if ya lucky." Then she smiled suggestively.

Grayson looked up and said, "Sorry, I didn't mean to be rude but you are beautiful."

She smiled with an even bigger smile. "Thanks but my name's not beautiful, it's Nikki. What's your name, handsome?"

"Oh, my name's not handsome, it's Grayson. Nice to meet you too Nikki."

"It's nice to meet you too, Grayson. You're not from around here, are you, as I don't remember seeing a good looking lad like you in here before?"

"No, I'm originally from London, but I've moved here for work so I live in Sunderland now."

"Ah reet, okay. So ya a cockney then, living in Mackemland?"

"Yeah, I sure am and I plan to be around for a while."

"Ah okay, that's great. Well, how about we have a couple of drinks together and get to know each other then, gorgeous?"

"I'd love to but I'm really tired and really need my bed, so how about this; I'll pay for your next couple of drinks and we'll pick this up next time I see you?"

"How about I join you in your bed and I can keep you warm?"

"Not this time, beautiful but maybe next, but I will still buy you those drinks."

Nikki wasn't happy that he wasn't accepting her offer of a quick lay tonight. Either he was gay or he really just didn't want to have sex with her, but she would take him up on the offer of having a few drinks bought for her until she saw the next guy that would want to sleep with her.

"Hmmm okay then, your loss, sweetness and yeah, I'll take those drinks."

"Okay good, you enjoy the rest of your night and get home safely. Actually, here's twenty pounds to pay for your taxi to wherever it is that you live. Good night, Nikki."

"Yeah, goodnight, Grayson. Hope to see ya again soon and thanks for the taxi money." Even though she knew she had no intention of sleeping in her own bed tonight, not if she could help it anyway.

Grayson caught the attention of the girl behind the bar and gave her twenty pounds to put behind the bar for drinks for the beautiful young lady with blonde hair in the black dress, and the girl behind the bar nodded her head and said she would.

After this Grayson left the pub and made his way home. He couldn't be bothered to wait for food, so he would just get something when he got in the apartment. He'd bought some Pringles with his groceries, so they would go along with a glass of water before he went to bed. By the time he got into bed, it was nearly midnight and he was ready to pass out as the call of sleep was shouting his name.

Grayson woke up the next morning, got out of bed feeling good, and his stomach started to growl. This morning he was going to have a bacon and egg sandwich, orange juice, and an apple for breakfast. After he'd made his breakfast, ate it and read the paper that was delivered every morning, he decided it was time to take a shower then get ready for whatever he'd planned for the day. Maybe even a drive to Ryhope to see what it looked like and then maybe on to a place on the map that he saw was called Seaham, which again was further along the coast.

While getting dressed, Grayson liked to keep the television on so he could hear what gossip was going in the entertainment world from the morning television shows. Whether it's about the Kardashian clan or one singer having a feud with another over their love life etc., for Grayson, it passed the time and filled the silence in the room when he wasn't playing music from his phone through the speakers of his television. Something caught his attention as a news special bulletin cut the TV show off. "This just in. The body of a young female has been found at The City of Sunderland Rowing Club at the early hours of this morning. Details have not been given to the public yet as it is now part of an on-going investigation. Eyewitnesses from the rowing club said that the young lady had blonde hair, blues eyes and she had a tattoo on her wrist with the name of Joanne." This made Grayson turn to look at the television as the description given sounded like the young lady he was talking to last night at the pub. "Anyone with any details please call this crime stoppers number 0800 555 111 or your local police station. Now back to your local programming."

He couldn't believe what he had just heard on the news. He opened his laptop quickly and it seemed like forever for it to load up and be ready to use. Grayson opened up his search engine and entered www.sunderlandnow.com to see if there had been anything put on there yet. There was but it was just the same as what had just been on television five minutes ago. All different thoughts started running through his head like would they think he done it? Would they find out that he spoke to her last night and left money for her behind the bar?, Would he be a suspect?, Should he call the police station and tell them that he saw this lady last night in the pub? If he brought her home, would she have been alive now? Should he throw away the clothes he was wearing yesterday in case they find any of her DNA on him? Would they think he had killed her? If he did throw away the clothes, would they think he was hiding something? What to do, what to do?

Grayson was now panicking as he didn't know what to do next. He started to think to himself, *"Don't panic Grayson, you didn't do anything wrong. Take a few breaths, relax and decide what you're going to do next".* The trip to Ryhope and Seaham was going to have to wait as now he had a problem, a big problem, and he needed to decide what the next step was going to be. He could either call the police station or crime stoppers or just get in the car and go to the police station and tell them what he knew. Hopefully, they won't see him as a suspect just someone that had seen her the night before, bought her some drinks, left her money for a taxi, and then left by himself. What would clear him would be if the pub had cameras on the inside and out. Then they could see that he left on his own and went home.

Chapter 6

It was Natalie's day off so she was going to do some detective work of her own. She'd heard that another body had been found and it'd had similarities to the other two murders that she had been sent to. The same as the other two, this lady was young and in her early twenties. The only difference with this body was that there was a possible name with her as there was a name tattooed on her wrist. That was three young women that looked very similar, discarded in the same way, and also the fact that they were all found along the River Wear. She started wondering if there had been more bodies found further up the river and wondered if any reports had been filed with Durham Constabulary or any other police for that matter.

There was a friend at the coroner's office that had sent Natalie an email with copies of the autopsies of the three young ladies. If her friend had been caught, she'd certainly have been fired and probably arrested. Natalie printed out the three files she had been sent and it was like looking at the same autopsy three times. It shocked Natalie to the core.

From what Natalie could tell from the notes that she had made was that all three had died of strangulation and had been dead eight hours or less before being found. There had been no sign of sexual assault but semen was found on the body possibly post-mortem. All three girls had blonde hair or dyed blonde hair, and all three had blue eyes. No restraint marks were found on the wrists or ankles, so it showed that they had gone willingly or they knew the person that had taken them. What she did find strange was that the cuspid tooth or the bottom right canine tooth of all three ladies was missing. Natalie wondered if this was the thing that the killer had taken from each of his victims. If this was the case, then there was a possibility a serial killer was in the area, and he had to be stopped.

Natalie had contacted her friends that worked on the Durham police force and asked them if they would check and see if there had been any unsolved murders along the River Wear that ran from Wearhead. She had given her friend the description of the young ladies that had already been found and wondered if there was any similarity in their area. Natalie's friend said he would call her back with any information that he could find and told Natalie that if he did, she would need to go to CID and advise them that she had found a connection but not give any names as it could get them into trouble, and she agreed not to mention any names.

It only took her friend, Michael, an hour to get back to her regarding the information she'd asked for. What she'd been told had made her, and also Michael, speechless. There was a serial killer in the area. Michael had found another four with the same description that she had given him. The first had been at Croxdale Viaduct of a young blonde, earlies twenties, who had died due to asphyxiation. She had no restraint marks on her but she did have a tooth missing, the bottom right canine. The second body, again the same as the first but was found at Maiden Castle footbridge, the third at Elvet Bridge, and the fourth was found at Prebends Bridge. All in the water as the killer must know that it would affect any evidence that would be collected or the time of death, as they didn't know yet if the killer kept them before he/she disposed of the body.

She thanked Michael for the information, but now she was wondering if she should check nationally and see if this killer had been active in any other areas. It seemed to her that the killer was local as he/she knew where the bridges and viaducts were that ran along the River Wear, so she doubted she would find anything nationally.

After getting off the phone with Michael, she walked the floor a few times as it was now sinking in what she had just discovered and how serious this really was. Either Captain Cynthia Harris of CID was going to be pissed for Natalie going off the books and investigating without prior approval, or she was going to be impressed with the work she had done and she would get to follow this case through to the end.

The day was going over pretty fast as Natalie had looked over the details in front of her and then rechecked everything in case she had missed anything. Any DNA or forensic evidence was still at the lab, so she couldn't include or exclude anything from those results until she could get her hands on them— and that could be a problem as she didn't know anyone that worked in the labs that would let her know or email her any results.

Lauren was working late tonight, so Natalie decided she was going to order take out as she couldn't be bothered to cook anything. She didn't know if she could possibly eat something, even though she knew she had to at least try and eat and relax for the rest of the night. She didn't want Lauren to see what she was working on, so she picked everything up off the floor and put them in a case file to take to work the next day; she would need to go in earlier so that she had the chance to speak to Captain Harris before her shift started. If Lauren had seen what she'd been working on, she would freak out and demand Natalie find a new job. Lauren didn't like Natalie being a cop as it put her in danger, and she didn't want to get the call that something had happened to her, but she also knew that Natalie was proud to be a cop like her father. It was eleven-thirty p.m. when Lauren got home from work and was tired but decided to take a shower before going to bed.

That night Natalie had nightmares and all she could see were the faces of the young women that had died, and they were shouting, "Help us, please somebody help us!" and screaming. Natalie shot up out of bed sweating and then remembered what the rookie had said to her, "I always wondered if people that have been, ya know, murdered or have taken their own life or the people that have died in car crashes etc., if they stay grounded here because they have some unfinished business or don't even know that they've died if it was sudden." And that made Natalie shake as she wondered if they were trying to tell her something or that she was missing something.

Lauren woke up at the same time and looked at Natalie and asked, "Nat, are you okay, what's wrong?"

Natalie hadn't noticed that Lauren had woken up and was looking at her with concern on her face. "It's okay, just a bad dream. Sorry, I woke you. Go back to sleep, I'll be okay. I just need a drink of water," and she smiled.

Lauren wasn't convinced "Okay as long as you're sure you're okay," and she watched as Natalie got out of bed to go and get a drink.

"I'm sure I'm okay baby, please just lay back down. I'll be right back, I promise." Lauren lay back down and went to sleep.

Natalie walked out of the bedroom, went to the kitchen and got a drink of water then gulped it down quickly. The next moment she knew she shouldn't have done that as she was now running for the bathroom and brought up all the water she had drank and more. She took a few breaths and went back to the kitchen and sat for a while so that her stomach could settle. She looked at the clock on the wall and it said that it was only two-forty five a.m. so she knew she had time to go back to bed for at least another couple of hours before she had to be up again for work.

When the alarm went off at six-thirty a.m., Natalie didn't want to get up but she knew she had to, so she kissed Lauren on the cheek then got up. Lauren wasn't at work until mid-day so she could have a sleep in and be okay for work. By seven a.m., Natalie was ready to leave, so she went back in to say goodbye and I love you to Lauren and then left. Natalie had all the paperwork she needed as she had a meeting with Captain Harris as soon as she got into work and she was feeling pretty nervous about how it was going to go. She got a coffee and a sausage and egg sandwich on the way in to the station so that she would be fully alert and ready for any questions that came her way.

It wasn't hard this time in the morning to find a parking spot, but when she started on later shifts it was impossible. She parked the car, gathered her things and started the walk to the third floor to CID but to Natalie, it seemed like it took forever to get to where she needed to be. When she finally arrived she spoke to one of the detectives, told him her name and that she had an appointment with the Captain. He smiled and told her to take a seat and that he would let the captain know that she was here and that it shouldn't be too long. Natalie started to get nervous again and wondered if the coffee and sandwich was going to come back up, but as soon as she was thinking this she heard a women's voice and at first it didn't sink in what has been said until she looked around and saw a lady of great stature standing in front of her and she said, "PC Roberts, hi, I'm Captain Harris. Nice to meet you. I hear you wanted to speak with me about something you have found."

Natalie was absolutely stunned by the lady that was standing in front of her, so she stood up, shook her hand and replied, "Yes, yes, I'm PC Roberts and yes, I need to speak to you about something. It's nice to meet you too".

Captain Harris smiled back at Natalie and replied, "Okay, let's go into my office and we can talk. If this lasts longer, then I'll make a call and let your Sergeant know that you'll be with me for a while."

"Okay thank you, that's very nice of you." Natalie replied.

Captain Harris smiled, "You're very welcome. Please take a seat and let's get started with what you have. I'm very interested."

With this being said, Natalie calmed down and took the paperwork and everything that she had and put them out on the table. Captain Harris made her feel really comfortable and asked one of the detectives to please get them drinks while they spoke and went through what Natalie had brought with her.

"Okay, PC Roberts, what do you have to show me?" Captain Harris asked.

Natalie looked at the Captain and said, "Where do I start?"

Captain Harris smiled at Natalie and said, "Start at the beginning, dear and we'll go from there, shall we?"

Natalie felt very relaxed now so she started, "Well…

Chapter 7

It was five-thirty a.m. and Grayson's alarm was going off telling him to get up for his first day at work at the RVI. He was quite looking forward to his first day and what it was going to bring. He was going to try and get there early, so he could look around and get the layout of the hospital in his head so that he wouldn't get lost if he was sent somewhere. By six-fifteen a.m. he was showered, dressed, picking up his messenger bag, wallet and keys to walk out the door. The metro station was a short walk so it wouldn't take him long and the metro was due in a few minutes.

Once he was on the metro he'd found a seat and put his headphones on and started to listen to music as the metro went from station to station. Grayson hadn't realized that thirty minutes had gone by and he was now approaching his stop, Haymarket, so he quickly put his headphones away and stood up ready to get off the train. Once he got off the train he followed everyone else up the escalator and out of the train station. After crossing the road he then started making his way towards the RVI and began to mentally prepare himself for his first day in his new job. If it was anything like his job in London, he was going to like it here and the days were going to go over fast.

The weekend before, Grayson had driven his Mercedes to Ryhope and driven around the streets to see where his mother had grown up. Ryhope was an old coal mining village, and if he'd studied it correctly then his grandfather had worked in those exact coal mines once upon a time. He'd done some research on the internet and found that his mam's family were quite well known for something called marching jazz band which he'd never heard of before apart from the American bands. Apparently, his grandmother and her brother had started Ryhope Allstars Jazz Band up in the early 1960's and it was still going strong to this day through his grandmother's children and grandchildren. He'd found a few videos on YouTube of them and he thought they were great. Apparently, they go to different competitions each weekend then have a big championship later in the year. Grayson didn't even know this world existed and there were bands all around the country that competed. Once he got to know his family, then maybe he might go to see them.

Ryhope was a nice little village, Grayson thought, and he might eventually move here when the time was right. He drove through Ryhope Village which had a war memorial right in the centre of the green which he assumed was a memorial from the World Wars. He then drove further into Ryhope and he noticed there were quite a few pubs here. He continued driving and found himself at Tunstall Village then into Silksworth. When he reached this point, he turned the car around and drove back into Ryhope then pulled the car over to take a look around.

As he started to walk down the main street, he noticed that people were looking at him, like they already knew that there was a stranger in their little village that they didn't know. Even though they didn't know him, they still said hello and went on their way either pushing their babies in pushchairs, people walking their dogs, or simply people walking to the stores to go shopping. Just like the bottom of Ryhope, the top of the Colliery as it was known, had its own fair share of pubs. He was certain that if people weren't at work or home, then they were in the pub. One weekend night he would come back and check out the nightlife in Ryhope and see what it was like.

After having a good walk around and seeing everything he could see, he decided he would go back to his car and head towards Seaham which was also a coal mining town and apparently, from what he found online, this is where the band practised on a Sunday afternoon if they weren't at a competition. Seaham was also along the coastline and wouldn't take him long to get to from Ryhope. When Grayson got to Seaham, he'd spent a little time there and found a nice place to have something to eat and a drink. After finishing his meal, he walked along the seafront for a while as it was a nice day and he was enjoying the beautiful views of the North Sea along the coast.

Grayson didn't realize what time it was and he was starting to get tired, so he made his way back towards his car and went home. He had to get up early the following morning for work so tonight was going to be an early night for him, but he promised himself that he was definitely coming back here as he enjoyed how relaxing it was and how peaceful it felt. Tomorrow was going to be anything but relaxing and peaceful for him, he thought to himself.

The beginning of his first day at work was all paperwork and getting his employee badge made, being taken through the employee handbook regarding safety in the workplace, the do's and don'ts and last but not least the code for what you could and couldn't wear for work. Grayson has already been through all this in London and he knew it so didn't give it much attention. He just nodded and said okay to make it show like he was listening.

When he got back to the wards, he was busy for the rest of the day doing rounds, changing dressings and also helping to do discharge papers for patients that were heading home. He was pretty happy with his day's work and the doctors that were on duty were also impressed with his work ethic and knew he was going to fit in just fine with the other doctors, and the patients were going to love him. The end of the shift was coming up soon and the night shift staff were coming in and getting handover details of patients that would be in overnight and what they had to be aware of. Grayson just had to listen to how it was done and realized it was the same as London but didn't want to say anything in case it was taken the wrong way. He said his hellos and goodbyes to the night staff and made his way to the changing room to get changed into his street clothes. As he was leaving he could hear the nurses, female and male, and doctors talking about him so he just turned, smiled, waved then said his goodbyes yet again. Now it was time to walk back to the metro station and get home.

Once Grayson got off the metro at Sunderland he realized how hungry he was and decided tonight was a pizza and beer night as he was tired after his first day. Tomorrow was bound to be the same again. He was sure after a week or two he should be on top of everything and aware of where everything was, and he could start getting comfortable with his surroundings. Once Grayson picked up his pizza, he started making his way home but had a weird sense that someone was watching him. He didn't know where from but he definitely felt it. He looked around himself a couple of times but didn't see anything.

While walking through the town, he started to think about the poor girl that had been murdered maybe hours after he had spoken to her. He still felt a little guilty about not letting her come back to his place that night. She had said that her name was Nikki, he wasn't sure about that, but then he'd found out that she'd had a tattoo on her wrist with the same name.

He'd decided that he was going to contact the police when he'd found out what had happened to her and went to the police station to give a statement so they could rule him out as a suspect even though they would still be watching him very closely. He'd told them that he'd met her in the pub and that he'd put twenty quid behind the bar for drinks for her and that he'd given her a further twenty quid for a taxi so that she could get home. He also told them that after this he said goodnight then left, he would be seen on CCTV leaving, and went to get something to eat before heading home. What Grayson didn't know was that after he left the pub, the girl followed him out a couple of minutes later in his direction. The bar staff and the cameras verified this and he couldn't believe it, but Grayson had a card up his sleeve that the cops didn't know. When he moved into the building, he'd put hidden cameras on the inside and outside of the front door and also the inside and outside of his flat door for safety that would show that she definitely didn't come back to his flat that night. He could show them right there and then and give them a copy of it as it was run through an app on his phone which at the moment he was thankful for. They let him leave not long after that and told him to stay in the area in case they had any other questions.

By the time Grayson got home, he was ready to collapse in bed and go to sleep, but he really needed to eat and drink something before he got into bed. He switched on the television but wasn't really watching it because he was so tired. He still couldn't knock the feeling that he had been followed, so he would check his cameras tomorrow when he had a chance and see if anyone showed up behind him after he'd walked in his front door.

Again tomorrow was going to be an early day as he'd rather be early to work than late. He could sit and relax a little in the doctors' break room before it was time to set foot on the wards and have another busy day, which he didn't mind in the least because it was something that he enjoyed doing, and the doctors, nurses, and patients were great and that made it a lot easier. Grayson knew it would be different when he went to Accident and Emergency and not everything would be that straightforward or easy, so he was going to enjoy this while he could.

Chapter 8

The meeting with Captain Harris had gone really well for Natalie and she would be allowed to follow the case with the exception that she was to contact major crimes immediately if any new information was to come up. Captain Harris was going to get all forensic, blood and fingerprints results, as she told the captain that was one thing she didn't have, which made Natalie happy. The Captain advised Natalie that she would be assigned as a PC to the Major Crimes Unit until this case was finished. Captain Harris had told Natalie that when they were alone she was allowed to call her Cynthia and this reminded her of what she had said to Peter on his first day with her. Peter would be partnered with someone else until she went back but then she didn't know if she even wanted to go back as this is where she truly wanted to be.

Cynthia had jumped into action as soon as she'd finished reading everything that Natalie had brought to her and was very impressed with what she was seeing. If this case went well then she'd be keeping Natalie right here and making her a part of her team. The team could do with a few more women like Natalie on the squad, instead of it just being her. The detectives on her squad were really good and worked well as a team, so she was interested to see what putting a female in the mix would do. If she knew her guys, and she hoped she did, they would welcome her and listen to what she had to say.

Natalie went home that night the happiest she'd been for a while and realized she was finally starting to get where she wanted to be, and she couldn't keep this from Lauren any longer. Tonight when Lauren got home they were going to celebrate a little with a good meal and a couple bottles of beer, or for Lauren it would be wine which she could pick up on the way home with the ingredients for their meal. When Lauren got home from work, she couldn't hold it in any longer and told her the news.

At first, Lauren was shocked at what she was hearing as she now realized what the nightmares Natalie was having were about. She wasn't happy to hear that Natalie had been following a possible serial killer in the area, but when she heard that Natalie had gone to CID and they were now going to take over the case, it eased her worries and concerns but it still worried her that Natalie was on the case and not back to what she was doing. She could see the excitement in Natalie's eyes and didn't want to make a big deal out of it, so she congratulated her and asked her to please be careful and listen to what the captain and the detectives were saying and follow their lead. Natalie agreed to this and now they could sit and enjoy the meal that Natalie had cooked for them and the glass of wine that had been put out for her. Today had been a hard day for Lauren and when Natalie had asked how her day had gone, she'd just said it was a busy day. Thankfully the next day they were both off work and they could sleep in and relax or maybe go out for a little, as they hadn't done anything together for quite some time due to schedules.

After a good night sleep, they both woke around midday and decided they were going to go out to South Shields. They could do some shopping then maybe spend some time on the front relaxing and have a couple of drinks or even go on a few rides at the fair if they felt like it. Natalie thought this was a great idea as she could do with a day of not thinking about work and spending the day with Lauren was the perfect thing to do, no matter what they decided to do.

Lauren had made them breakfast and it had been a full English breakfast which included eggs, bacon, sausage, toast, tomatoes, beans and a nice fresh cup of coffee. After eating their breakfast they decided it was time to take a shower then make their way out as it was already two p.m.

Lauren decided she needed a new pair of trainers and Natalie decided she needed a new pair of jeans, so they looked around and found what they wanted then bought them and took them back to the car. After dropping their shopping off, it was still nice and sunny so they decided a walk along the beach would be nice. They walked hand in hand along the front before heading towards the fair to see what rides would be open. They both enjoyed the rides so they decided to go on the AtmosFear, Miami Surf, the roller coaster, and some other rides. By the time they had finished on the rides it was starting to get late and they both had early starts the next morning. Natalie loved to see Lauren smile, having fun, and this made her heart melt as that is all she ever wanted to see and she loved Lauren's smile and everything about her. They made their way to the car and Lauren decided she wanted some cotton candy for the drive home, so Natalie bought her some and watched her take every bite.

By the time they got home, it was ten p.m. and nearly bedtime. They'd gotten pizza to bring home so they didn't have to cook anything since they were both now tired from the rides. The next few days were going to be busy for Natalie so she made the most of spending every second with Lauren that she could. They had sat down in front of the television when they got home to eat a slice or two of pizza, but Lauren couldn't keep her eyes open and fell asleep on Natalie's chest. Natalie loved to hear and watch Lauren as she was sleeping, even if she did snore a little, but she didn't mind at all as it was comforting and it reminded her that she loved her even more than she did the first day she'd met her. She woke Lauren up and moved her to the bedroom where she could take off her clothes and get into bed. It didn't take long after this that Lauren was back to sleeping peacefully after the day of fun they'd had.

Natalie wasn't quite ready to settle so she decided to check out her social network sites and see if anyone was doing anything new or had any new announcements they wanted to share. Usually, there wasn't anything new but people bitching or moaning about someone else, or someone complaining that their life was so bad that they had to broadcast it. None of this interested her and she kept out of it as it would bring nothing but trouble which both Natalie and Lauren didn't need. If anyone had anything they needed to know then they could contact them personally and not over a social network where everyone could see. She had finished with that and signed out of the website before she opened up a new window and loaded the local news to see if anything new was happening.

When Natalie opened the local news website she couldn't believe her eyes. There had been another body found but no details had been given and nothing about where it had been found. She couldn't decide whether to call in to find out what had happened and see if this murder was connected to the ones that she knew about. She was hoping that they would contact her if there were any new developments regarding the case but then she was new to major crimes so it was a big possibility that they wouldn't.

The more she thought about it though, she had brought them the case so she expected the courtesy of being kept updated. Natalie tried refreshing the page to see if any new details by magic would show up, but to her disappointment, nothing new came up.

It was just past eleven-thirty p.m. when Natalie decided that she had better go to bed and get some rest as tomorrow was definitely going to be a busy day. She closed down the laptop then made her way towards the bedroom. While she was getting undressed her mind was going crazy with questions about this latest murder and she wondered if it was even connected to the ones that she had taken to major crimes. It didn't take long for Natalie to fall asleep before the nightmares were starting again, but she'd tried to ignore them; otherwise she was never going to get any rest.

It had felt like she'd just closed her eyes to go to sleep when the alarm started going off and she slammed at it with her hand to shut it off. Lauren woke up with the sound of the alarm and cuddled into Natalie, but she had sensed that something was wrong as Natalie didn't respond to her,

"What's wrong, baby?" Lauren asked.

Natalie, turned to look at her and said, "There's been another body found, but I couldn't find any details about it."

"Oh no, do you think it's connected to what you found?"

"I don't know. I guess I'll find out when I get to the station."

"Ah okay. Well, come and have a shower with me; we can leave at the same time and you can fill me in about it tonight if you want to. If you don't, then I understand. All I ask is for you to be careful and stay safe as I don't know what I would do if anything happened to you."

"I will be careful, baby, don't worry. I will join you for that shower too. Let's do our part for nature." Natalie said smiling and they both made their way towards the bathroom.

Thirty minutes later they were both just getting ready when Natalie's phone began to ring and she answered it immediately. It was Detective Stephens who she had been partnered with to work CID. He'd told her to make her way in as there were some developments in the case and they had a lot of work to do. Natalie knew the developments he was talking about, and the body found last night must have been another to their list. She told him she was on her way in now and would be there in twenty minutes.

Detective Stephens was a great cop and he'd been on the force for at least twenty-five years, ten of those with CID so she could learn a lot from him and learn some new tricks to the trade. However, she did wish it was under different circumstances.

Natalie kissed Lauren and they said their goodbyes as she got in the car and Lauren was making her way to the metro station to go to work. She hated being apart from her love, but she knew that they wouldn't get anywhere if they were both unemployed and spent every minute together in bed. Although it was a nice image to hold on to as she pulled away from outside of their house and made her way to the station.

When she got to the station Detective Stephens was already waiting in his car for her and sounded the horn as soon as she got out of her car so she didn't go into the station first. The car horn shocked Natalie and she didn't know who it was at first, but then she recognized the driver and saw that it was the detective blowing his horn at her. Today was the first day that Natalie got to wear smart dress clothes for work, but when she got in the car she noticed that Stephens was just wearing jeans and a black top which made her feel overdressed. Stephens was in his mid-40's but he was in good shape and she noticed he took pride in his appearance.

"Get in the car, probie, we haven't got time to waste." Stephens shouted not realizing that Natalie was already in the car.

"Okay, no need to shout. I'm not deaf, but I think I may be now. Where we going anyway? And my name isn't probie, it's Natalie."

Stephens smiled "Oh okay sorry about that. I thought you were further away than you were, and you are probie as you're new to the team and everyone in the team will call you that for a little while anyway, or until somebody else new comes into the team. We are going to the scene of the latest murder to see if it fits our killer's modus opperandi and then onto the coroner's office to get the results from the autopsy. Is that okay with you, probie?"

Natalie blushed a little and replied, "Yeah that sounds great to me, so let's get moving and see what we have. What are you waiting for?" Natalie said with a cheeky grin and off they went. Yeah, they were going to get along just fine.

Chapter 9

After a very long day on a sixteen-hour shift, Grayson was ready for his bed. He had been on-call that night and it went over pretty quick apart from a quiet spell around three a.m. This time was spent in the on-call doctors' room trying to catch up on some sleep, but that never happened as Grayson didn't like this room. He made a mental note to try and rent a place very close by so that he could go and rest, take a shower, and also have a proper meal instead of snacking on crisps and chocolate. If he was called back, then he could be back within minutes if he ran.

This shift had been the shift for broken hips, legs, and wrists which he didn't mind as each took a few hours to put back into place and then stabilize with a cast. The broken hips would need to go to the operating theatre as they couldn't be put back into place while in the emergency room. One case that came in was of a pregnant lady who had been run over by a car and had multiple injuries. Subsequently, a team from the Delivery Suite had been called as the lady had gone into early labour and the team of midwives, OB/GYN doctors, and healthcare assistants were on hand if they had to deliver the baby. Luckily the baby had not been harmed when the mother had been knocked over by the car and the heart rate was good, but the same could not be said for the mother.

Grayson had caught the eye of one of the midwives and she was smiling at him, but at the time he was concentrating on the patient and trying to stabilize her fractures as no surgeries could be done until the lady was stable. The Delivery Team moved the lady to the Delivery Suite and Grayson was told to be ready in case he was called to the Delivery Suite if things got worse. The midwife gave her number to him and he said he would be on-call for the next few hours and would be available if needed. The piece of paper he was given with the number on said that the midwife was called Alison and she would be looking after the lady whatever the outcome.

When his shift ended, he went up to the Delivery Suite to see how the lady and the baby were doing, but it wasn't good news. The lady had been intubated and heavily sedated, but the sedation was also affecting the baby. It's heart rate started to get dangerously low so they decided the best option was to do an emergency cesarean section to try and save the baby. The baby came out limp and was rushed to the special care baby unit to be taken care of. The mom was taken back to the room and has being watched very carefully, soon to be moved to the intensive care unit where she could be closely watched, but fingers crossed they would both survive. Grayson asked the midwives to keep him informed on the status of mother and baby then said his goodbyes and left to get changed to go and catch the metro home.

While riding home on the metro, Grayson felt like he was been watched and looked around him but didn't see anyone looking at him, so he just pushed it off and called himself paranoid. Maybe it was just because he was tired and exhausted but he was almost sure he was been watched. While waiting for his stop, he checked out this morning's news on his phone to see if there was anything worth reading about, but as soon as he saw about another body being found, his jaw nearly hit the ground. Something really bad was going on around the city, and he said a silent prayer for the poor lady that had now lost her life.

All this talk about life and death made Grayson think that there was no time like the present to reach out to his mam's side of the family and let them know that he exists. When he went to see them he decided he was going to take photos of his mam and records to show who he was and that he was their relative, as he had a feeling that some may not believe him and think he was trying to con them. Grayson was off for the next couple of days so he would ask if one or two of them would meet him or if he was brave, he could just go and knock on the door of one of his aunties and explain who he was and see if they would be willing to talk to him.

When he finally reached Sunderland station he exited the metro and decided he would pick up a coffee and something to eat before he went home to sleep. He'd forgotten how hungry he was until he thought about food and his stomach started to remind him that he needed to eat something. On his way home he decided, for now, he would get a couple of sausage rolls from Greggs the bakers and pick up a coffee at the same time. When he got up in a couple of hours he would make something better to eat and then decide if and when he was going to contact his family.

It was nine-fifteen a.m. by the time he got to bed. He figured that a couple hours of sleep would be okay, so he set his alarm on his phone to go off at two p.m. and then take a shower when he got up. It was five p.m. when he woke up and realized that he must have slept through his alarm as he hadn't heard anything. He must have gone into a deep sleep as he hadn't heard his phone ring either, but there was a voicemail and he wondered who it was from. He got up out of bed, went to the bathroom, washed his hands then went to start the coffee maker. While waiting for the coffee to brew, he pulled an orange juice out the fridge and then went to retrieve his phone to find out who had called. There were actually two voicemails and the first one was from his father.

"Hi, son, was just wondering how things were going as I haven't heard from you in a while. I just wanted to see how you were and how the new job was going. Things are going well here. I miss you. You know you could always come back and I can get you your job back at the hospital if things are not going as planned. Give me a call when you get a chance so that we can have a catch-up. Talk to you soon son. Bye." Part of the message from his father made him angry as he automatically assumed that things weren't going well. He would call his father later when he'd had the chance to calm down.

He went on to the second message that had been left. "Hi, Doctor Shaw, this is Alison calling from the Delivery Suite at the RVI. You wanted to be kept up to date regarding the lady and baby that had been hit by a car. The baby is doing well in the Special Care Baby Unit, but unfortunately, the mother passed away an hour ago due to organ failure and the injuries she had sustained. Her husband is here for the baby so the baby won't be alone. Just thought you should know. Have a good day, Doctor Shaw, bye." This had made Grayson very sad as he'd had high hopes that both would pull through and have a full recovery. He also felt sad for the husband and new father who now had to bring up their child by himself.

Grayson took a cup out of the cabinet and poured himself a fresh cup of coffee. He had some bagels in the cupboard that he'd bought, so he put one in the toaster until it was done, put some butter on, and ate it. After eating and drinking, Grayson decided it was time to take a shower then maybe go out for a little. Possibly to Ryhope to see what was going on as he noticed on social media that some of his cousins were out with their friends at a karaoke competition tonight, and he would have the chance to see what they were like.

The night in Ryhope was a great night and Grayson was having a great time. He had managed to sit along with his cousins and their friends just after he had got there, and they were crazy but fun crazy. The more they drank, the crazier they got. He'd found out that his cousins were called Natasha, Tricia, and Devon, and they looked like they were having fun. Natasha was the quiet one but loosened up after a couple of drinks. Tricia was all fun, loved karaoke, and sang a lot with Devon. Devon seemed to be the sober one and he loved karaoke too and so did their friends. Grayson at this time decided he was going to approach Devon and pull him to the side and see what he would say to the news of having a long lost cousin that they didn't know turn up and be sitting in the pub with them.

Grayson was feeling very nervous as he didn't know how this was going to turn out after he'd told Devon who he actually was. He decided for Dutch courage he was going to have a couple of Southern Comforts to ease the nerves, but it didn't seem to help. Devon was standing at the bar by himself getting another round of drinks for himself and his sisters when he decided it was better now than never, so he approached and said to himself out loud, "Here it goes. All or nothing."

"Hey Devon, are you having a good night?"

"Oh hey, Grayson. Yeah, I'm having a great night, how about you? I'm just getting a couple of drinks for Tash, Tricia and myself. Would you like one?"

"Ah, no thanks, but I would like to have a chat with you in private if that's okay. I have something important to talk to you about."

"Ah okay, gimme a minute to give my sisters their drinks then I'll be with you okay? You're not gonna ask if my sisters are single are you, as I don't get involved in their personal lives with guys."

Grayson looked and smiled at Devon. "No, no, nothing like that. It's about something else that you may find interesting."

Devon looked at Grayson with a questioning look "okay, gimme a minute to put these drinks down and then I'm all yours."

Grayson nodded his head in response and waited for Devon to return. He could see that Devon was telling his sisters that he wanted to have a word with him and they looked past Devon with their own questioning look and wondered what it was about.

Devon came back five minutes later. "Okay, I'm all yours, where do you want to go?"

Grayson saw an empty set of seats in the back corner where it was quiet and pointed to Devon to where he was looking at. "Over there would be good," and Grayson led the way.

Devon looked at Grayson as there was an awkward silence between them, but he didn't know that Grayson was struggling with a way to start the conversation.

"Okay, Grayson what is this about? We've been sitting here for ten minutes now and it's starting to feel a little weird."

"I'm sorry, Devon; I'm just trying to figure out how to say what I've got to say. Okay, I think I have it." Then Grayson drank his drink in one go when he was ready.

"Okay, what is it you have to say?"

"Do you have an aunt that was called Tracey?"

Devon frowned at Grayson. "Yeah I do, but she moved to London when I was just a kid and we never heard anything from her until about a year ago when she rang my mom and said she was sorry for leaving the way she did and to please forgive her. She was planning to come up and see her with her family a couple of months after, but she never came."

Grayson didn't know that she was planning on coming to see her sisters and brother. "Ah right, okay, what can you tell me about her?"

"Not much really as I was so young but my mam had said that Aunt Tracey had gotten into some trouble with a man and that he used to beat her. So one day she gathered what she could and she left for London to try and start again."

"Ah okay, that makes sense. Why did the man used to beat her?"

"I don't know, do I? As far as I'm aware the man was a nasty piece of work and when he was drunk he used to beat her if she said the slightest thing wrong or did the wrong thing. Apparently, he used to call her all the names under the sun and all she said was that she was sorry."

"Is this man that beat her still alive and if so, where does he live?"

"He died about six months ago of liver failure from all the drinking I suppose."

"Ah okay, well it couldn't happen to a better person if that's the case"

Devon looked confused at his comment and couldn't figure out why he was asking about an aunty he knew very little about. "I know you're not from around here because of your accent, but can I ask you, why are you so interested about an aunty that now lives in London?"

Grayson had to prepare himself for what he was about to say. "I'm asking because Tracey died in a car accident about a year ago, and I'm trying to find out more about her and where she grew up."

"You're lying; she didn't die in a car accident. Surely her family would have let us know that this had happened."

"I'm telling you now."

"Wait a minute, what? What are you to my aunt Tracey and how do you know that she died in a car accident?"

"I am her son, Devon, and your cousin."

"No way, what, are you yanking my chain?"

"Yes way, I am Grayson Taylor Shaw and my mam married my dad a year after she'd moved to London. I'm here to figure out what had happened to my mam before she left as nobody ever told me and it was never spoken of. I only just found out that I had aunties, an uncle, and cousins that never knew I existed, so you can imagine what a shock it was to me."

"Yeah, I bet it was a shock as it's a shock for me now. Well, I guess you don't know that you have a half-brother, then do you?"

"I have what?"

"Yeah, you have a half-brother and his name is Graeme. We don't really see much of him these days as he seems to keep to himself. This is gonna be a big shock for him too."

"Oh wow, sorry for sounding stupid, but how do I have a half-brother if my mam came to London herself?"

"Two years before she left, she claimed that the guy had raped her and they had a son. Nobody believed that he'd raped her and they thought it was consensual. Apparently, she couldn't stand looking at her son as it always reminded her of the rape, so she left him with his father when she left for London."

"Ah right okay" This news was making him understand why his mam had left the area and relocated to London where she had met his dad. It was sad to think that if this didn't happen, then he wouldn't even exist on this planet.

Devon could see that Grayson was having trouble taking this news in. "If you want, I can arrange for the family to meet up at my aunties, sorry our aunties, and you can get to meet everyone in person. There are many other cousins you haven't met yet, and I'm sure that they are all gonna be shocked when they get to meet you."

"Yeah, that would be great, thank you, Devon. I have to work the next four days but after that, I'm free for a couple of days. Whenever you can get them together then I'll be there."

"Okay cool. Leave me your number and I'll give you mine, then I can send you the details of where to meet."

"Okay, sounds good to me. Will Graeme be there do you think?"

"I very much doubt it as he doesn't like family gatherings, so you may have to do that yourself in person."

"Okay, no problem. Thank you for your time, Devon. Let's go back to the others and you can fill in your sisters about our conversation unless you want to wait until they are sober." Grayson smiled when he said this.

"I'm sure once I tell them this they will sober up pretty quickly. It'll be like dropping a bombshell on them." Devon said laughing.

"Oh, I'm sure it will. Okay, let me get you that drink and we'll go back. Again thank you, Devon. This has meant a lot to me."

"You're very welcome, cousin," Devon said laughing "It's a Jack Daniels and coke for me thanks, you better get yourself a double."

"Yes, definitely a double for me."

Grayson was struggling to take in everything he was told but pushed it to the back of his mind and enjoyed the rest of his night with his newly found cousins and friends.

Things were starting to look up and now he's got that part out of the way.

The parts that shocked him the most were that his mam had left this area because some man was beating her and she had to get out of town.

The biggest shock to Grayson was that he had a brother who he knew nothing about, and he wondered if he knew anything about him.

Chapter 10

So you've made your way to Sunderland then, dear cockney wanker of a brother. Yeah, I know about you. I've known about you since you were a teenager and you started using social media. I actually came down to London a couple of times and was going to reunite with my mam, but then I saw her with you and your father and that filled me with rage as I never had that; so why should you? I was left with a drunken bastard of a father that beat me nearly every day because he blamed me for my mother leaving.

He used to always say that I should have been killed at birth as I was a waste of breath, useless and unworthy. It should have been you that was never born, dear brother. I should have had my mam and dad together. They should have been going to parents' evenings at school and seen how well I was doing, or for my case how badly I was doing.

I have been waiting for the day that we would meet and I would make you pay for taking my mam away from me. All I remember of my mam thanks to you is her beautiful hair and her eyes. I have pictures of her but that's not the same as having her in my life and having someone to go to when I had a problem. Sure, I had my mam's family, but they never understood what was going on and they never understood me.

I bet you never knew that I caused the car crash that she died in did you brother? Yeah, I was in the other car that ran her car off the road and made it roll over. If I didn't have a mam then neither would you, and you would feel some of the pain that I felt. Do I regret killing her? No, not at all, as like my dad used to say about beating her, she deserved it, and she deserved to die in the car crash as she left me then had you.

I have a secret to tell you, dear brother, but firstly what do you think of our beautiful area and the surrounding areas? The sights along the River Wear are beautiful, aren't they? Do you know that feeling when you feel like someone is watching, but you don't know who it is when you look around and don't see anyone? Well, brother, I'm the one that has been following you everywhere you go. I know where you have been and I know where you work. I was the one that night that had come in with a broken wrist and you put it back into place, then got one of those beautiful nurses to put a cast on me. You never gave me a second glance and that pissed me off. I was going to say something then but changed my mind and thought I would savour it for another time.

Oh, you must be wondering what the secret is. Well, do you know all those dear women that have recently been found along different parts of the River Wear? Well, I'm the one that killed them, dear brother, and I especially enjoyed killing that lovely lady that you had been talking to in the pub that night. I'd seen her following you when you went home that night. Wasn't she beautiful? But then she looked a lot like our mam, didn't she? So did all the other girls that I have killed and had pleasure during and after the fact with, let me tell you. I took a souvenir from each too and I'm planning on making a necklace with the canine teeth that I have.

I'm sure at some point you'll want to meet me, but unfortunately for you, it will be on my terms and not yours. I see you have already met three of our cousins; aren't they a delight? Not my cup of tea, but I'm sure you'll fit right in.

Oh, before I forget, let me tell you. Every time that I was strangling the life out of those beautiful ladies, I was thinking of you.

Chapter 11

Things were moving like a cyclone in CID since the latest body had been found, and they didn't know if and when the next body would turn up and be reported.

The DNA results were due back any day now from the DNA that had been found on the bodies, but it was very little each time so they were hoping that from what they did have, they would get a result, and maybe even get a suspect. Natalie had a good feeling about this and was keeping her fingers crossed as this could be a big break in the case.

Natalie was loving working in CID, and Captain Harris was a great boss. She was learning a lot from her and also from the detectives she was working with.

She hadn't really seen much of Lauren this past week as they were both busy and were working opposite shifts to each other, but Natalie knew there was something bothering Lauren but she couldn't figure out what. Was it something to do with the case she was working on or was it something to do with her work? To be fair she just didn't know, but she was definitely going to sit Lauren down and ask her what was going on. At the moment her concentration had to be on catching this killer, as his or her number of deaths was up to eight and he or she may not be finished.

The latest victim had been found at the Roker Pier Lighthouse, right where the River meets the North Sea, and the body was the same as the others apart from that, she had been badly beaten as if the killer had lost control and it looked like every bone in her face had been broken. For some reason, he'd made this one personal and it could be his own undoing.

A phone call had come into CID from dispatch that a woman matching the description of the other female victims had managed to get away from a male next to the River Wear. He had been trying to strangle her, but she fought back and had managed to get away, then someone that had been passing by had called the police. Natalie and her partner, Detective Stephens, had been asked by the captain to go and get a statement from the lady. They had to get as much detail as they could and hopefully have the lady sit down with a sketch artist so they could get a look at this killer to get out to the public so they could be on the lookout for this man. Natalie and Detective Stephens met the lady that had just been assaulted at the hospital as she'd had rope marks on her neck and some bad open wounds on her legs where she had scrambled to get away. She had been lightly sedated but she was still able to talk for a short while with Natalie. She had asked Detective Stephens to wait outside as the lady might be too traumatized to talk with a man there. Natalie had been made aware before she went into the room that the victim had been placed on 24-hour suicide watch just as a precaution.

Natalie interviewed the young lady, but she was only half making sense. She told Natalie that she was walking to the store and the next minute she was grabbed from behind and then hit with something across the back of the head. When she came round, there was a rope of some kind around her neck and the guy was muttering something that she couldn't make out, but he sounded pissed at whoever he was talking to. When she was fully aware of what was happening, the rope was getting tighter and she'd started to fight back and fought for her life. When she'd got enough space between herself and the guy, she had managed to grab and twist between his legs, which made him lose his grip, and she made a run for it. He ran after her, but she'd seen someone coming along so she ran to the passer-by and asked them to help and call the police.

She gave Natalie a brief description of what the guy looked like;- about five feet nine inches, in his early thirties, quite muscular, about a hundred and seventy pounds, clean shaven, short light brown hair, and blue eyes. Natalie had asked if she would be able to describe him to a sketch artist, and she told Natalie that she would be able to but not right now. Natalie said that was okay but she would be in contact with her in case they needed more information. Natalie had given her a card with her number on just in case she needed to talk or if she remembered something that they needed to know, and the lady agreed.

When Natalie walked out of the room, Detective Stephens asked if she'd managed to get anything useful. Natalie gave Stephens her notes to look through and he was happy with what he saw. The Captain would definitely be impressed, and they would have plenty to work on and see if there were any cameras in the area that caught all of this in action.

By the time they got back to the station, it was 6 p.m. and it had been a long day. Natalie decided before she went home she was going to write up the report from the interview she'd had with the most recent victim, who, surprisingly, was still alive. Two police officers had been placed outside of her room just in case this guy decided he wanted to finish the job he'd started. Not many detectives were left in the office as they'd already gone home for the evening, but Captain Harris was still there and obviously waiting for Natalie and Detective Stephens to come back. Natalie had told Stephens to go home to his wife and kids as she was going to do the report and she would give a run-down of what happened to the captain.

Captain Harris was definitely impressed with the details that Natalie had given her, and she was going to fight to keep Natalie right here when this case finished. She saw a younger version of herself in Natalie. She ordered Natalie to take the next day off and relax, as she'd worked hard since she was kept at CID. The captain told Natalie that she would get two detectives to go in and check on the victim tomorrow and another two would check cameras in the area. If anything new came up, she personally would call her to come back in, but she really needed Natalie to get some rest as she was starting to look tired and she needed her at one hundred per cent and focused.

After Natalie was finished with Captain Harris and had written the report, it was nearly nine p.m. She knew that Lauren was due to finish work at ten p.m. so she decided to drive to the RVI to pick her up as a surprise, and maybe they could go for a drink after she had picked her up. It was more than likely that Lauren wouldn't get finished on time, as working on the Delivery Suite was very busy and they had to do the hand over before she could leave. She would wait in Maternity Reception until Lauren came out the main doors from Delivery Suite. She knew the girls on reception, so she would just stand and talk to them for a while until Lauren was ready.

It was ten-forty five p.m. by the time Lauren came through the doors, but she was talking with a doctor who she recognized but couldn't place where she knew him from. Natalie hid around the corner until Lauren was walking past and said, "Hey gorgeous, need a ride?" and started laughing and smiling. Lauren was shocked but happy to see Natalie. She ran over to Natalie and started to hug her tightly and gave her a kiss.

"Hey, beautiful. What are you doing here, and yeah, I do need a ride." She smiled back.

Natalie looked at the doctor again and she realized where she remembered him from. "Hello Doctor Shaw, nice to see you again. I didn't realize you worked here at the RVI. Hope you're well."

Lauren looked at both of them with confusion as she didn't realize or know how Natalie would know Doctor Shaw. Grayson looked at Natalie and replied, "Nice to see you again too, PC Roberts. Yeah, I started here a few weeks ago and I am very well thank you. I hope you are doing well too. I was just up here getting an update on a patient that was pregnant that had come through the Emergency Room."

"You don't have to explain anything to me, Doctor Shaw, I'm just here to surprise my girlfriend and take her home, which I don't do often enough." Natalie smiled at Lauren.

Grayson was starting to feel nervous so he made his excuses to leave. "Ah right, okay. Well, I'd better be getting back to the Emergency Room. Have a safe ride home and enjoy the rest of your evening." Then he left.

Natalie saw that he was leaving and said, "Thank you, Doctor. I hope you have a good night too and safe travels home to you too."

Lauren looked at Natalie again with confusion on her face and was waiting to see if Natalie would explain how she knew the Doctor, but nothing came so she finally said, "Well?"

Natalie looked at Lauren "Well, what?"

Lauren wasn't enjoying this. "How do you know Doctor Shaw?"

Natalie wondered how long it would take for Lauren to ask how she knew the Doctor. "Oh, he was a person of interest in the case I'm working on."

"What! The serial killer case do you mean?"

Natalie looked around to make sure that nobody had heard what Lauren had said. "Keep your voice down, baby. That hasn't been released to the public yet and yeah, that case, but Doctor Shaw has been cleared so there are no worries. Okay?"

Lauren took a breath and a look of relief was on her face. "Phew, okay baby."

It was eleven p.m. by the time they had left the RVI, so Natalie and Lauren decided they were just going to head home and pick up some fish, chips, and mushy peas since they were both starving by now. When they got home, they ate their food and drank a bottle of water each. Natalie decided this was the perfect time to ask Lauren what was bothering her and see if she could help.

"Hey baby, I have something I want to ask you. Over the past couple of days, even weeks, you seem to be walking around with something on your mind, and I just wondered if you wanted to tell me what was wrong?"

"Oh, there's nothing much really. I guess I just miss our time together, and one of the girls that was killed, I knew her. We weren't really close, but we had gone to school together and it had just made me sad. That's all, baby."

"Why didn't you say something to me, baby? We could've talked about it. Nothing specific about the case but we could've talked. I'm sorry I haven't been around much lately, but we are determined to catch this killer so nobody else gets killed."

"I know you are, babe and I'm very proud of you. Don't you worry about me, I'll be okay, and the service for the girl is tomorrow if you feel like going with me."

"Of course I worry about you, and if you would like me to go, then I will, but the rest of the day you are mine my beautiful, gorgeous, sexy and amazing woman."

"Yes, my love, and then I'm all yours."

"Okie Dokie, that sounds like a plan to me. Now, my love, it's time for bed."

"Why are you tired, babe?"

"Who said anything about going to sleep?"

"Oh babe, naughty, naughty, but let's go." and off to bed they went.

Chapter 12

Today had been uneventful at work for Grayson so he'd gone to the Delivery Suite to see what was happening there and see if he could be of any use. When leaving, he wasn't expecting to bump into PC Roberts at Maternity Reception. She had come to see him about the girl that had died and took the statement from him. Grayson had been taken into an interview room where she had come in and asked him a lot of questions. Seeing her again made him a little nervous and he wondered why she was here but, then he noticed that she wasn't even looking at him but the midwife that he was walking out with. Grayson said his pleasantries and made a sharp exit back to the Emergency Room. When he got back a stabbing victim had come in, so he made himself busy with his patient.

Grayson finished his shift at midnight and made his way straight home as there wasn't really anything happening at that time of night apart from drunken people coming out of pubs. Tomorrow was going to be a big day as he was about to meet his mother's family who he'd never met before, and that made him nervous. The one person he wanted to meet was the brother he never knew he had, and he wondered if he was anything like him or their mother. When he got home from work he decided he was just going to have something quick to eat and drink then go to bed. Today had been a long day again for him and all he wanted was his bed.

When Grayson woke up the next day it was just approaching nine a.m. He decided he was going to say in bed for a little longer and rest before he got up. He turned the television on in his bedroom and watched a little of the morning shows but quickly lost interest, so he got his laptop to see what was happening on social media. He tried to keep in contact with his friends down south, but they seemed to be busy doing other things or going on travels to other countries. He would love to do it himself one day but this wasn't the right time to do it.

By eleven a.m. Grayson had eaten breakfast, had coffee and orange juice, took a shower, got dressed and was then ready for the day that was ahead. Today was going to be a big day for him and he told himself to expect the unexpected, because to be fair, he didn't know what to expect at all. When he got the text from Devon it said that he was to meet everyone at the Oak Tree Farm pub and restaurant in Doxford Park and they were going to meet at one p.m. He'd never been there before, but he texted Devon back and said that he'd be there. Before he left he put the name of the pub into his maps on his phone and got directions so that he wouldn't get lost or be late.

Grayson left his apartment at twelve-thirty p.m. which gave him plenty of time to get there. He picked up his keys and wallet and made his way out to the car. It was a pretty cloudy day, but he still decided against taking a jacket as he wouldn't be spending much time outside. It was forecast for rain later in the day, but he figured he would be home before that even began. Grayson got in the car and set his phone up so that he could follow the directions and by that, it said it wouldn't take him long to get there. He felt strange as he had no nervousness about meeting them, but he was sure he would when the time came to say hello to his family.

He got to the Oak Tree Farm with ten minutes to spare, so he decided to go in and find an area where they could all sit and chat without being disturbed by other people. Grayson bought himself a diet coke; he really didn't like drinking at all while he was driving, so diet coke it was. Five minutes later, Devon walked in with his sisters and also who he assumed was his mother. She had a look of disbelief on her face when she saw him standing up from his seat and couldn't believe that this was Tracey's son who she had never met. A couple of minutes after they had arrived, the rest of the family arrived and gave him the same look as Devon's mother. Grayson knew what each of them looked like due to looking at them from their social media accounts, but in real life, they all bared a resemblance to his mother which knocked him back a little as his mother's face showed up in his mind. Devon's mother must have been Kate, the older lady must have been Margot, and the youngest of the three must have been Sarah. The gentleman that came in with them was obviously Brian. When everyone got sat down Devon,

Natasha, and Tricia went to the bar to get everyone drinks before they got comfortable and began to talk.

The talking started and at first, it was all about his new family wanting to know all about Grayson Taylor Shaw. Where was he brought up? Who was his father? Where did he go to school? Did he have a good relationship with his parents? Did he go to college and/or university and if so where? What did his father do for a living? Where did he work in London and where was he working while he was in the area? Was he married? And did he have any children?

Grayson answered all of their questions but the majority came from his aunt Sarah, as she seemed the most inquisitive. He was brought up in Kensington, North London, his father was Patrick Taylor Shaw and he was a plastic surgeon. He told them that he went to the City of London School, he had a great relationship with his parents, he went to The London College of Osteopathic Medicine, he worked at King's College Hospital which was part of the NHS Foundation Trust and he was a Consultant while he was there. He was currently working at the RVI as an Orthopedic Surgeon and no, he hadn't been married or had any children. Grayson was waiting for more questions but none came until his aunt Margot asked how their sister had died and when? He informed her that his mother had died in a car accident and it had been about ten months ago. He informed them that he had actually brought some of her ashes with him so that he could spread them in her hometown and she could finally be at peace.

After more questions and answers, they decided it was now time to have something to eat and refresh their drinks. Everyone seemed happy with the answers they had heard, and Grayson was sure that there would probably be more which he didn't mind. The questions that struck Grayson were the ones that his Uncle Brian asked, which was if his mother was happy, what she did for a living, and did she have a good life? These were easy questions to answer for Brian as his mother had been very happy, she had been a housewife, and she definitely had a good life up until the accident.

Time had gone past quickly and it was nearly five p.m. by the time he looked at his watch. He'd enjoyed the meal and the company but now he was starting to get tired. He had found out a lot about his mother and the things she used to get up to when she was a kid, and it actually made him laugh trying to imagine his mother getting into trouble and then getting the belt when she got home. He'd found out more about the bastard that used to beat on his mother, and he wasn't happy with what he heard. Apparently, the guy called John was older than his mother and he'd met her in the pub. They said that he was very strict and wouldn't let her go anywhere unless he was with her as he got jealous very quickly if another guy came anywhere near her. If a guy looked at her, then she would be beaten and told that she had been beaten because she was flirting with other men and it was her fault. He expected his breakfast, dinner, and tea ready at specific times otherwise she would be beaten again, and again, and again.

They had said to Grayson with deep regret in their voices that when Tracey had come to them and said that John had raped her, they hadn't believed a word she'd said as she kept going back to him. Little did they know at the time that she had actually become pregnant, and Tracey didn't want her son growing up without a father. The family also didn't realize that that would have been the better option because when Tracey left, John had started to beat on his son. He would be seen in public with black eyes, bruises, and split lips. Graeme had become a recluse when his father died and stopped seeing any of the family. When anyone went to the house, he wouldn't let them in or he would simply ignore them.

Grayson definitely wanted to meet his brother, but by the sound of things, this wasn't going to be easy by any means of the word. Maybe he could get him to meet him at the pub instead of his house so that he didn't think he was intruding. He asked Devon if he had Graeme's number so he could either call or text to set up a time and place to meet. Devon had said to Grayson to not hold his breath as he probably won't answer, and the best way to catch him was when he went out to buy more drinks at the local corner shop. Grayson nodded his head in acknowledgement.

By the time they said their goodbyes, hugs, and kisses, it was six-thirty p.m. and Grayson was tired and just wanted to go home and think about everything that had been said then go to bed. Before he went to sleep he decided to send Graeme a text to see if he was willing to meet and if so where. He was hoping by the time he woke up tomorrow he would have an answer, but he wasn't counting on it.

Everyone that he had met was very nice, pleasant and welcoming as if he'd known them all his life and not just since that afternoon. He promised to keep in touch and maybe go to see the marching jazz band next time he was off work. He wasn't at work the next day but he wanted to give himself some time to go over what he had learned and think about how he was going to fit in here. Tomorrow he wasn't going out anywhere, so he would just stay in and watch whatever was on television or watch a couple of movies depending on what was available on Netflix.

It was only nine-forty five p.m. by the time he got into bed, but he was so tired he figured tonight was going to be an early night. The only problem he had was that he had so much running through his head that he wondered if he was going to settle at all. He turned off the lights and the TV and surround sound speakers then just lay in the dark. Grayson stared into darkness then said to himself, "Wow, what a day," and instantly fell asleep.

Chapter 13

Captain Harris wanted the attention of the whole squad as she had something important to tell them. She had been busy the last few days because of the case that PC Natalie Roberts had brought to their attention.

"Listen up everyone, stop what you're doing and listen," she shouted.

Everyone stopped and looked at her as she normally didn't give big speeches, so everyone knew this was going to be important.

"Okay thank you." she continued. "I have an announcement to make. Due to the case that our lovely PC Roberts brought to us, we now have international attention and especially from across the pond." Natalie looked at Captain Harris and everyone else and blushed at the spotlight that was now on her, but Captain Harris moved on.

"I have been in contact the last couple of days with the FBI and they are interested in the case and have offered to send a special agent over to help us with the case. I have taken up this offer and the agent will be here tomorrow, so Roberts and Stephens, you will be going to pick up Special Agent Sharp from the airport at seven a.m. okay?"

Natalie and Stephen looked at the Captain and answered, "Yes Ma'am," and put on American accents. Luckily for them, the Captain found this funny and gave a little laugh.

"Roberts seeing that this was your case that you brought to us, you will be sitting in on all meetings with the special agent and filling in any blanks that I may miss. Stephens you also will be sitting in on meetings as you have been working with Roberts, but before you do, I would like you to make sure that the other detectives have their assignments and that they will be ready to help out on this case if needed."

This time they both answered with, "Yes Captain."

Cynthia Harris decided now was as good a time as ever to run through everything with Natalie to make sure all the facts were in order. The DNA tests had come back, but there was nobody on file to connect a suspect and nothing had come upon the Automated Fingerprint Identification System or AFIS for short. Cynthia had even tried putting some detectives undercover in case anyone of interest happened to show up in the pubs in and around the area, but to no avail.

The next morning Natalie and Detective Stephens were at Newcastle International Airport at six-thirty a.m. watching and waiting for the connecting flight from Paris, France to arrive with Special Agent

Sharp on it. Natalie was excited to meet an FBI Special Agent and this was her chance to prove that she was good at her job. Stephens wasn't as excited. He thought he didn't need an American to come in and show him how to do his job, but he wasn't going to voice his opinions as it was the Captain that had invited the Special Agent in, and if it helped to catch this serial killer, then he would see what they had to say.

While they were waiting, a report had come over their phones that a body had been found, but this time it was of a young male, in his early thirties, light brown hair, about five foot eleven inches tall, muscular build. This didn't sound like their serial killer and they sent a message asking why this had been sent to them. It came back that the young male had been strangled and the body had been found just under the Monkwearmouth Bridge in the water of the River Wear. It had also been noticed that the bottom right canine was missing in the young man's mouth, which connected it to the case. Two other detectives had been put on the case, but a full report was expected to be given to Captain Harris and Natalie Roberts.

Both Natalie and Stephens were wondering why the killer had gone for a male this time as it had all been young females before. It didn't make sense to them why all of a sudden the killer had gone from female to male and this had both of them scratching their heads trying to understand it. Maybe the FBI agent could make sense of it all.

While waiting at the airport, Natalie and Stephens drank coffee after coffee as they had been up extremely early to make their way to the airport. It was now seven a.m. and on the arrivals board, it said that the flight from Paris was on approach. It would take maybe twenty to thirty minutes to get through arrivals and collect luggage, so they both took a seat for a little and Natalie put the board down that had the Special Agent's name on it so that he or she knew who was here to drive them to the station. Firstly they would drive the Special Agent to the hotel that had been booked so that he or she could drop their luggage off and get refreshed before going to the station.

On the arrivals electronic board it now said that the flight had arrived on time, so Natalie and Stephens got out of their seats and got themselves in a good position so that they could be seen as soon as you walked out of the arrivals door. Just then Natalie got another message, this time from Captain Harris saying, "Natalie drop the Special Agent off at the hotel and advise him or her you will be back later, or if plans change then tomorrow morning, and for them to relax and catch up on any jet lag that they may have. I need you and Stephens back at the station as soon as possible." Natalie frowned and showed Stephens the text then he frowned. Natalie texted the Captain back and replied, "Yes, Captain. May I ask why you need us as soon as possible?" The Captain replied, "Tell you when you get here. See the pair of you soon." This completely confused both of them, but they did as they were told.

As Natalie and Detective Stephens were waiting, the arrivals doors opened. A few couples walked past them as they must have been to Paris or somewhere for a holiday. Next through the doors was an average sized, muscular man with short cropped hair, and he was dragging his bag behind him. They both looked at each other and knew that this was who they were waiting for. As soon as the man saw them with a sign saying "Sharp," he started to smile and came straight toward them.

"Hi, I'm Special Agent Sharp. I take it you're my ride to the station."

Natalie smiled back and in response replied, "Hi, yeah we are. I'm PC Natalie Roberts and this," pointing to Stephens, "is Detective John Stephens. We are here to take you to the station, but there has been a change in plan. Captain Harris has ordered us to take you to your hotel, which is the Hilton Inn in Sunderland, and you can rest, take a shower and get over any jet lag you may have, maybe even order something from room service."

Sharp looked at Natalie and Stephens with curiosity "All right, I could do with a shower and something to eat. Can I ask why things have been pushed back until tomorrow, because if I'm correct, we have a serial killer to catch and I need to make a profile so we know who we are looking for?"

Natalie wasn't sure on how much to say so she left it to Stephens to reply, "Welcome to England, Special Agent Sharp. Captain Harris has given us orders and we are to return to the station as soon as possible. We are not sure why, but as soon as we find out, and if it's involved in the case, then I'm sure it'll be included in your briefing tomorrow with ourselves and the Captain. If you need anything while we are gone, then please give us a call and we'll do what we can to accommodate your request. Please enjoy the amenities of the hotel and we'll see you bright and early tomorrow morning."

Both Natalie and Special Agent Sharp were taken aback by what Stephens had just said and all Sharp could say was, "Okay, thanks."

As Natalie and Stephens left Special Agent Sharp in his room, she turned around and said "Sorry about that, and we'll see you at 8 a.m. tomorrow morning. Please enjoy your evening, Special Agent Sharp."

Sharp smiled at Natalie and replied, "Don't worry about it. I don't take offence easily and thank you. Please call me Andy, and I will see you in the morning, PC Roberts."

Natalie smiled as she was starting to close the door, "Please call me Natalie," and she closed the door and left.

It was just past noon by the time they got back to the station but Natalie and Stephens were curious as to why Captain Harris wanted to see them. When they stepped in the office everyone was busy and Captain Harris was on the phone but saw them and waved them straight into the office. They sat down and waited until the Captain got off the phone. It didn't take long for her to finish her call, and she finished whatever she was writing, then looked straight at Natalie and Stephens.

"Did Special Agent Sharp have a good flight from DC?" she asked Natalie.

"Yes, Captain. He did and he is at his hotel relaxing right now."

"Okay good. That was actually him on the phone. He wanted to know if we could send him some of the files so that he could start working on the profile, but I advised him to rest and he can start on it tomorrow."

"Ah right, okay good. He's eager to get started. That's good to know."

Captain Harris didn't really like sensitive files on open cases leaving the office where anyone could see what they were working on; Special Agent Sharp was no different and he would have to wait until the following day to see the files as he would need to be briefed on the cases and what they had so far.

The Captain had a look of concern on her face and both Natalie and Stephens didn't know why, so Natalie asked Cynthia, "Is there something else that we need to know about, Captain, as you seem to have something on your mind?"

Cynthia looked at her notes and then realized that she hadn't explained about the latest murder victim and that it was a young male and not a young female.

"Oh yes, I meant to update you regarding the latest victim. As you know this is a young male that was found at the Monkwearmouth Bridge. You were sent the description regarding this male, but I recently just got the crime photos in from the scene. The young gentleman was killed exactly the same way as the young ladies, and I have made sure that all DNA and any other lab results come straight to me as we need all the information we can get."

Natalie asked the Captain, "May I see the crime scene pictures please, as I would like to see them and all paperwork from the officers and detectives that responded to the scene?"

Cynthia looked at Natalie and replied, "Of course you can. I have everything here for you to look over and see if you see anything that I have missed. Please come, we can go into the conference room and look over everything there with everything else. You too, Stephens, as you might see something that we are not seeing."

They all stood up and left the Captain's office and made their way to the conference room, Captain Harris first, then Natalie and then Stephens. Stephens saw that the other Detectives were still very busy with what they were doing, and if they found anything or heard anything regarding this case, then they would bring it straight to them to be looked over.

Stephens closed the door behind him. He hadn't realized how much work had actually been done on this case already, and the majority by Natalie herself. He was really growing fond of this young lady, and he would be proud to be her permanent partner if the Captain decided to keep her with them.

Cynthia Harris took out the paperwork and the photos from a file that had been delivered and placed it all on the long clear glass table that was in front of them. They had their work cut out for them and by the looks of it, it wasn't going to be an early night as every piece of evidence had to be scrutinized and looked over meticulously so nothing would be missed.

Cynthia called in an order for take away, as she was sure that both Natalie and Stephens would probably be hungry since they probably hadn't eaten yet, and also very strong coffees all around as they had to stay alert so that they wouldn't miss anything. All the confirmation she needed was the sound of Natalie and Stephens' stomach rumbling very loudly so she left them to look over the evidence while she went and placed the order herself.

When she went back into the conference room she noticed that Natalie was staring at a picture of the now deceased young man and wondered if she knew him. "Are you okay, Roberts? You look like you've seen a ghost."

Natalie didn't realize that Cynthia had spoken until Stephens nudged her in the shoulder and moved his eyes in the direction of the Captain. "I'm sorry, Captain, I didn't hear you. What did you say?"

Cynthia, still looking at Natalie, replied, "I said, are you okay, Roberts? You look like you've seen a ghost."

"I'm sorry, no, I haven't seen a ghost, but these pictures of this young man remind me of someone that we know, and we have interviewed him in connection to the case. I actually saw him not long ago at the RVI and that's where he's working."

Cynthia was confused whom she was talking about, and Stephens didn't know who she was talking about either, so she asked, "Who are you talking about Natalie, and who is it that works at the RVI?"

Natalie took her eyes away from the pictures and brought her head up to look at the Captain and Stephens. "These pictures look a lot like Grayson Taylor Shaw. We questioned him when the young woman with the name Nikki tattooed on her wrist was found the day after he was seen in a pub talking to her."

"Do you think that it's him, Roberts?" asked Stephens.

"No, I don't think so, but he looks very much alike," Natalie replied.

Cynthia looked at both Natalie and Stephens with a questioning look. "Okay, both of you go to Dr Shaw's address and see if he's there. I'll get one of the other detectives to call the RVI, see if he's at work, and get some background information on him. If he's there, then bring him in for a little chat and we'll see if we can piece this together."

"Yes, Captain," they both responded. They grabbed their things and made their way out of the office and to the car. Natalie was hoping that it wasn't Grayson, as she knew this would be hard on Lauren if it was. Natalie looked at Stephens and said, "Okay, let's get going," and Stephens started the car engine and off they went.

Chapter 14

It had been a long night and Grayson had only been in bed for an hour in a deep sleep. He thought he'd heard knocking in his sleep, but soon awoke when he realized it wasn't in his dreams but his actual front door. Whoever it was that was banging on his door was banging real hard. Do they not know that he'd just got in from doing a sixteen-hour shift at the hospital?

He slowly got out of bed and put on a t-shirt and a pair of shorts then slowly made his way to the door. If the person knocked any louder, then there would be no need to answer the door because the door would be off its hinges. Whoever it was, he wasn't going to be happy with them as Grayson was exhausted and really needed some sleep. As he approached the door he shouted, "Okay, I'm coming, I'm coming already." When he reached the door, he took the locks off and opened it. He was shocked to see both PC Roberts and Detective Stephens standing there, and it woke him up pretty quickly.

"Hello, PC Roberts and Detective Stephens, how can I help you?"

"Good morning, Doctor Shaw. We would like you to come to the station with us, so we can ask you a few questions. Do you have time now to go to the station?"

"What, right now?" Grayson asked "I just got off work an hour ago after a 16-hour shift and I'm tired. Can I come down after I have some rest?"

Natalie thought about it, but Stephens replied, "Yes, right now Doctor Shaw as we have some important questions that need to be answered."

Grayson rolled his eyes. "Can you not ask me here, now, or does it have to be at the station?"

Natalie looked at Grayson and could see that he was tired, irritable, and needed sleep. "We would prefer it to be at the station Doctor Shaw. Please get ready and we'll wait outside for you. It won't take long then you can come back home and go back to sleep."

Grayson wasn't happy, but he couldn't really say no to their request. After all, they were the police. "Okay, give me a little time and I'll be with you. You can wait here in the apartment if you like and help yourselves to a drink. It won't take me long."

Natalie and Stephens gave a nod of appreciation and helped themselves to a bottle of diet coke each, which was cold straight out of the refrigerator. They took this time to take a look around Grayson's apartment while he was getting ready, but didn't find anything of any interest. Natalie walked over to the desk that Grayson had in the corner and noticed that it was all family information, so she assumed that he must have been looking up his family history. Natalie saw a pad with some writing on it and looked around her to make sure that Grayson hadn't come out of his room yet, then she looked back at the writing pad to see what he had written. Natalie noticed that at the top it had a title of "Family Members" and a whole list of first names, where they lived, what relation they were to him. While Natalie looked down the list one thing caught her attention and that was of Grayson's brother, but he hadn't written a name there yet.

Just as they had finished looking around Grayson came out of his bedroom and was ready to go. He noticed that they must have been looking around as they were both in different areas and turned around when he walked into the room. He had nothing to hide, so he was confident that nothing could be used against him.

Grayson looked straight at Natalie with a questioning look and she just smiled and said, "Are you ready?"

Grayson smiled back and replied, "Yeah, I'm ready. Just waiting for the both of you to finish snooping around."

Stephens came up to Grayson and said, "Well, let's get going. We have very little time and plenty of questions for you to answer."

Grayson smirked at the pair and answered, "Okay, I'm ready when you are. Let's get this over with so I can get back and get some sleep." All three started making their way towards the door and Grayson picked up his keys, wallet, and phone then set the alarm on the door as they left.

When they got to the station Natalie showed Grayson into the interview room and got him a strong coffee. While he was waiting in the interview room, Natalie asked one of the other detectives to find out what they could about Grayson's background and his family history since last time they spoke to him they didn't have much about him as he was only giving a statement about seeing the young women in the pub before she died. This time Natalie was going to have all the information she needed. Before she went into the interview room she noticed that Captain Harris was in her office and speaking to someone quite heatedly, and it made her wonder who it was but that wasn't any of her concern as she had to concentrate on speaking to Doctor Shaw. Captain Harris would probably tell her if there was a problem she needed to know about.

As she walked into the interview room one of the other detectives ran up to her with all the information she needed about Grayson's background, which would come in useful if it was needed. Just then Stephens came up and was ready to go into the room with Natalie. As they walked in Grayson was falling asleep in the seat but woke as soon as the door opened. He looked at both Natalie and Stephens as they pulled the seats out and sat in front of him then put a file down on the table.

Natalie started the conversation by asking Grayson if he needed another coffee and he just nodded his head. Whoever was behind the mirror would bring one for him. Five minutes later a knock sounded at the door and a detective came in with another coffee. Natalie was ready to start so she asked Grayson, "How are you doing, Doctor Shaw?"

Grayson looked at Natalie and replied, "I'm okay, just tired. Can we please just get on with this and get the questioning done so I can go home to my bed? And please call me Grayson. Doctor Shaw makes me sound old, and that's what everyone calls my father."

Natalie smiled, "Yeah sure, let's start. Okay, Doctor Shaw, sorry, Grayson. Can you tell me a little about yourself and why you moved from London to this area please?"

Grayson gave Natalie and Stephens the whole story about why he had moved to Sunderland and about the death of his mother. How he had just found out recently that he actually had family in the area, and that's why Natalie had found all the details regarding those people on his desk at home and also that he had just recently met them. He also let them know that he recently found out that he had a half-brother who he hadn't met yet, and he had sent a text a few days ago but never got any reply.

Stephens asked the next question, "Can you tell us anything you know regarding the recent murders that have been found along the River Wear?"

Grayson found this a strange question, for why would he know anything regarding them unless they thought that he was a suspect for these murders? "Do you think that I committed these murders, because I didn't. I'm about saving lives not taking them. If you are going to treat me like a suspect, then maybe I should have my solicitor here and not say another word."

Natalie looked at Stephens with an angry expression and then back at Grayson. "No, no, Grayson, we are simply just asking the hard questions first, but it would help us if we knew where you were when these murders did occur."

Grayson was slowly getting agitated by the questions, and the tone of his voice changed. "You want to know where I was. Well, for the majority of the time I was either working, in my apartment, in a pub, or not even in the area, so please feel free to check. Even better, please check the GPS on my car or even the videos from CCTV of when I get the metro to and from work. I can give you a copy of my schedule of when I work at the hospital too, if you like."

Natalie and Stephens knew that the atmosphere was turning tense, so Natalie tried to lighten the mood. "Personally Grayson, I don't think that you are the suspect, but I have the feeling that someone around you is trying to put the blame on you." Natalie stopped to take a breath and to give Grayson a chance to think about what she had just said. "Do you know anything regarding the recent murder, Grayson?"

Grayson looked shocked at Natalie. "No, I know nothing of any recent murder or any of the murders, just what I hear on the news. That's how I learned about the young woman I had spoken to in the pub, and I called to say that I had spoken to her the night before and to give the information. I feel sorry for every young woman that has died and the person that has actually killed them needs to be locked up for the rest of their life. As I said before I'm about saving lives not taking them."

Natalie looked at Stephens and he nodded his head for her to carry on, as she was getting further with him and getting more answers. "Okay, Grayson, this is going to be a bit of a shock, but the latest murder was actually of a young man which brought us to you. We didn't think it was connected to the young women until the body was examined and we noticed some similarities to the women."

Grayson was shocked that there had been another murder, of a young male this time, but he was still confused on how this had anything to do with him. "Ah okay, well, I didn't know there had been another murder, and for the past three days and nights I have been at work which you can check. Still, what has this got to do with me?"

Stephens took over and answered Grayson's question, "Well Doctor Shaw, it seems that whoever this killer is, he was thinking of you, as the young man that is dead could have been you or a twin since he looks like you. At first, we thought that it was you until we came to your door and you answered. So we thought we would bring you in just for questioning and to see if you knew why someone would kill someone that looked like you."

Grayson couldn't believe what he was hearing and thought that he was in some awful nightmare. "No, I don't know anything about any young man that had been found, and he really looks like me?"

Natalie nodded. "Yes, he does, very much so. I saw the crime scene pictures of the young man, and even I thought it was you as I had only recently seen you at the hospital and knew what you looked like."

Grayson rubbed at his face and couldn't comprehend what he was hearing. "Do you think that my life is at risk?"

Stephens responded, "We don't know, but we will be watching you in case anyone makes an attempt on your life." Grayson nodded his head in response but stayed silent.

Natalie asked, "Would you be up to giving us a DNA sample so that we have you on file." Grayson wanted to say no, not without a court order, but that would make him look like he had something to hide so he decided to just give them what they wanted.

"Yeah sure, whatever you want. I'd be glad to help."

Just then there a tap on the door and it opened. Another detective was trying to get their attention and by the looks of it, it was urgent, so both Natalie and Stephens stepped out of the interview room to find out what was happening. The detective that had come to the door advised them that another body of another male had been found in the river next to the Stadium of Light, and they were needed as soon as possible. They decided that there was no way that Grayson could have done this meaning that he definitely wasn't the suspect, but they would get the DNA from him anyway and keep it on file as reference.

They went back into the interview room and informed Grayson that they were finished and that he was free to go after giving his DNA. Grayson was happy that this was finally finished with and that he could go home. Natalie informed Grayson to stay in contact in case they needed him and that a patrol car would take him home if he wished, but he decided against it and decided he would walk home himself.

As Grayson was walking out of the station, he saw Natalie and Stephens running to their car and also some other detectives running to theirs too. Something must have been happening and this made Grayson wonder if there had been another body found. He couldn't decide whether to try and find out what was happening or just leave it alone. He decided on the latter and started making his way home. If they needed him, then they knew where he lived and worked and knew how to find him.

Chapter 15

Why did you have to try and text me, little brother? I'm not going to answer you and I have too much to do to answer you, like framing you, but then again, why would I want to do that and let you take the credit for my beautiful work? I hope you liked my latest work as that was just for you. He looked just like you, didn't he, and he could've been your twin.

I saw them take you in for questioning, so I left them another little present down in the river next to the football stadium. If they still suspect you after this one, then I guess I'll have to be more obvious about where I leave my bodies. Maybe one right outside of your door would be good. What would you think about that, dear brother, or how about I go for someone that you know personally, as that would definitely get your attention wouldn't it?

I have no intention whatsoever of speaking to you. I've never spoken to you before, so why would I now? Yeah, Devon spoke to me and said that you were interested, but unfortunately I am not. You have already stolen my mam from me, and now I am wondering who I can take from you as it would be you to blame for their death. Hmmm, how about that nice little midwife I saw you talking to a couple of weeks ago. She would be a good choice, don't you think, little brother? She doesn't fit my choice, but I would make an exception for you. Maybe after this one, then she will be next.

They will never find out who is killing these people since I'm too careful, but I get great satisfaction out of seeing the life draining from their eyes and faces. I know because I see it every time and make sure that my face is the last thing they see before they die. That one girl that got away was a problem as she saw my face, and the stupid fucking bitch, kicked me in the nuts which really fucking hurt. If that person didn't pass by, then I would have had her, but she was lucky and got away. I promise that will never happen again.

Maybe this afternoon I'll go out and find someone else. It's a nice day for it, don't you think, little brother? I always wonder if we were brought up together if we would be close and if we would be doing this together. Wouldn't that have been fun, brother?

Chapter 16

The next morning Natalie got the opportunity to see Lauren, and it made her realize how much she missed her, but at the same time how much she loved her too. They decided to stay and cuddle in bed for a little, but then they both had to get up and shower as it was an early start for the both of them. After showering, they ate breakfast together then got ready. Lauren started her shift on the Delivery Suite at seven-thirty a.m. so she would need to leave soon. Natalie held Lauren in her arms for a while then had to let go. Natalie had a busy morning herself as she had to go to pick up Special Agent Sharp from the hotel and take him to the station so that he could be briefed on the case and make his profile to help catch this serial killer. After walking out from their house, they said their farewells and went their separate ways.

Natalie was a little early, so she went to pick up some breakfast for Special Agent Sharp and also a couple of coffees for the drive in to the station. Today was going to be a very busy day for everyone and she wanted to see how Special Agent Sharp built his profile of the killer. He was going to keep in contact with his team in America as they were going to join in with some of the meetings by doing a video conference and give their opinion on what was going on.

While Natalie waited outside the hotel for Sharp she decided to send Lauren a text just to say she was thinking of her, hoping she had a good day, and if she got home tonight that they would spend some time together. She would check later for a reply as Sharp was coming out of the hotel and Lauren wouldn't be able to answer until later when she was on break, which was fine as she too was going to be very busy.

As they were driving to the station there wasn't much conversation. Natalie asked Sharp if he was enjoying his stay and if he had slept and ate well the night before. Sharp answered that yes, everything was good and that the food tasted different to him but he would get used to it and yes, he had slept very well. It didn't take them long to get to the station and once they got out of the car. Natalie showed him up to the office and straight to Captain Harris's office. The Captain asked Natalie to leave them alone in her office a moment and advised Natalie they would be in the conference room shortly to begin the briefing.

Fifteen minutes later the Captain and Special Agent Sharp walked in to the conference room and both seemed to be in good spirits after their chat, so Natalie assumed all was good and they got started on to briefing Sharp on the case. It took the whole morning and the best part of the afternoon to catch him up to speed, and he seemed happy with the information that was there. He asked to be left alone for a while as he was going to look over the details himself and video conference with the rest of his team in the states before giving his profile run down. Captain Harris and Natalie stepped out of the conference room to give him some space and also to grab a coffee. That's when Cynthia advised Natalie of what they had been talking about in her office. Cynthia told Natalie that her bosses weren't happy about bringing an FBI agent in on the case, and if this went south, then it would look bad on them and they would be the laughing-stock of the British police force. She had told her bosses that the case was going to be solved by them, and the FBI agent was only here in an advisory capacity. When she spoke to Special Agent Sharp this morning, he understood this, but he was very impressed with the amount of work that had already been done by themselves and especially by Natalie.

Natalie took this opportunity to check her phone and see if there were any messages or calls that she had missed from her beloved. She was hoping to see a text back from Lauren. There was nothing there from her although there were five missed calls from her work number, which she found strange and wondered why they would be calling her. There was a voicemail left on her phone but as she was about to check it, Cynthia shouted for her that they were wanted back in the conference room. Special Agent Sharp must have been ready to give his profile, so they grabbed their coffees and one for Sharp. Also by this time, Stephens was ready to join them, and he walked into the room with them to find out what the Special Agent had come up with.

Special Agent Sharp greeted each one of them as they walked into the room and welcomed Detective Stephens when he saw him and offered a handshake which Stephens accepted. Sharp must have finished and had his conference call with his team as the video screen was blank and switched off. He stood over the glass table with all the paperwork spread out in different piles so he must have been going through it piece by piece. Sharp asked all three of them to take a seat on the opposite side of the table from him and then he would start his profile, so all three of them obliged and sat. Natalie offered Sharp the coffee she had brought for him and he took it with a smile of gratitude, took a drink then put it down on the table.

Sharp looked each one of them in the eyes and smiled, but when he came to Natalie he smiled even more. "PC Roberts, have you ever thought about coming over to the states and becoming a behaviour analyst, because the work that I see here by yourself is very impressive." Natalie looked shocked at Sharp, then at Cynthia and Stephens, and with then back to Sharp. "No, never. All I ever wanted to be was a detective right here, as I never thought I would be up to the standard of this, never mind the FBI, but thank you."

Sharp smiled and added, "No, this amount of detective work is impressive and a lot of my colleagues don't do half the work that you have done here, and now obviously even more with the help of

Captain Harris and Detective Stephens. You have learned a lot in very little time. I would recommend you any day."

Natalie blushed then replied, "Thank you, Special Agent Sharp."

Sharp shook his head. "Please, as I said yesterday when you dropped me at the hotel, please call me Andy."

They all nodded in response and Natalie answered "Thank you, Andy."

Cynthia was bursting with pride for Natalie, but she was also getting tired of waiting for the profile. They needed that so it could be sent out to the other detectives and they could be on the lookout for this individual. She gave Andy the look as to say, "Okay, let's get a move on with the profile." With this Andy got started on his profile.

"Okay, I have spoken with my team in the states very briefly and we have a profile for you. We believe that the person you are looking for is a male in his late thirties or early forties. He is a social outcast and doesn't mix well with others, but we notice for him to be able to get so close to being able to strangle these victims that he can speak to women or even men and get his own way. He may use some sort of drug to control them, but if the victim was inebriated at the time, then he may not see this as necessary as they are already incapacitated. It's a possibility that in his childhood he was abandoned by his mother, father, or even both and suffered major emotional, physical, and mental abuse at the hands of the parent he was left with. He is an only child, because if there was another child, then he would have seen himself as the protector. However, it's very likely that he is the only child. He has traits of being psychopathic but also traits of been sociopathic. He lacks any kind of empathy for the victims and also lacks any kind of remorse. There is a high possibility that he is a high school dropout and lives within travelling distance to the crime scenes, so he knows the area well. His IQ is below average, so between eighty to ninety-five and he probably lives alone. His outward appearance would be irritable, restless, impatient, hot-tempered and disorganized. Last but not least, his motivation for killing would be for power, control, exploitation, greed, and most of all revenge. I hope that everything I have given you helps you to catch this individual. Are there any questions?"

Captain Harris, Detective Stephens, and Natalie all looked at Andy and were surprised he got all of that out of what was in front of him. Natalie asked that exact question and he responded, "Yes, I did. Serial killers follow certain paths and some invent their own way so that they can't be caught or be compared to anyone else like Ted Bundy, Jeffrey Dahmer, or the Son of Sam. They want to make a name for themselves and don't want someone else to take claim for their work, as that's how they see it. So, for your Serial Killer it would be that he likes to strangle his victims and take the bottom right canine tooth, which I have never seen before." Natalie sat with an open mouth and was astonished by what she was hearing, and by the looks of Captain Harris and Detective Stephens, they were feeling the same way.

Stephens had a question for Andy and it surprised everyone around him. "Is there a timescale for when he is going to kill again, because at the moment it seems like he waits a few days, but sometimes it's the next day and sometimes not?" Andy smiled. "Great question, Detective. However, he is trying to exact revenge on a particular person and it's spurring his killing. If he finds out that his murders are being investigated more closely, then he may increase his timescale or even the closer you get to catching him. It's a great possibility that the person that triggered this is also living in the area and he's watching them or even goes as far as stalking them and watching every move they make."

Stephens seemed happy with the response and replied, "Okay, thank you." Andy nodded and replied, "You're welcome."

There didn't seem to be any more questions, but Special Agent Sharp said he would stay around for a week or so or even until the case was closed, whichever came first. Sharp asked if they had taken any DNA from the gentleman that had come in for questioning and if the results had come in yet, and the Captain advised Sharp that they had taken DNA but the results had not come back yet but were due any day now.

While Sharp and Captain Harris were talking, Natalie took the opportunity to check her phone again to see if Lauren or anyone else had contacted her. There was still nothing from Lauren which started to worry Natalie as Lauren always sent a text on her break and even when she was on her dinner break, which, by now, would have been hours ago. This was starting to worry Natalie so she closed the messages on her phone and listened to the voicemail that had been left earlier.

"Hey, Natalie, it's Julie from the Delivery Suite. We were just wondering if ya know where Lauren is as she was supposed to be at work this morning and we can't get in contact with her. Hope everything is okay, and please get Lauren to call us as soon as you hear from her as we don't want her to get into trouble for not showing up for work. Okay, pet, speak to ya soon." Natalie started to freak out since she knew that Lauren had left for work that morning as they had left at the same time. She hung up from the call and began to call Lauren's phone, but it was going straight to voicemail, which was strange by itself as Lauren's phone was never switched off.

Cynthia and Sharp saw that there was something wrong with Natalie, so they made their way over to her to find out what was going on. Natalie explained to them that Lauren hadn't shown up for work even though she saw her this morning and she was making her way towards the metro station to go to work. Cynthia looked worried and so did Sharp, and they said they would pull all CCTV footage from the area and see if they could see Lauren on any of the footage. Natalie asked if she could leave to see if she was at home in bed or see where she was, and Cynthia told her to go ahead; they would contact her if anything came up. Sharp said he would use his laptop to try and track the GPS of Lauren's phone, but said it would be no use if her phone was switched off unless they could switch it on remotely. Natalie gave them the authorization to go ahead and ran out to her car. Stephens ran behind her and said he wanted to help, so they both left the station and made their way towards Natalie and Lauren's home to see if she was there. They both kept their fingers crossed that she was indeed at home and safe.

Chapter 17

When Grayson got home after being at the police station for questioning, it took him a while to settle, but he eventually had fallen asleep watching television in the sitting room. He was woken up by his alarm clock telling him it was time to shower and get ready for work. Luckily tonight was only going to be a short shift and he would only be there for eight hours; plus he was on the wards so it was more than likely that it would be a quiet night and he would get finished on time.

As he had thought, the night was quiet, so he caught up on some paperwork before he did his rounds of the patients with the other doctors and nurses. Then the patients would only be woken up if they needed to take their prescribed medication. He decided for tonight he would sleep in the doctors' room as he was too tired to care who had slept in the bed before him. He managed to sleep for four hours, and he felt a lot better for having that sleep. An hour before he was due to go home he made sure that the nurses didn't need anything from him. When he left, the only doctor that was available would be the on-call doctor due to staff cuts, and he was over on the other side of the hospital and he or she didn't know the history regarding these patients.

By the time he got home, it was four a.m. and the roads were clear. When he worked these shifts he always took his car as it would be easier and cheaper than having to get a taxi all the way home. The drive home gave Grayson time to think over everything that had happened the day before from beginning to end, and what a day it had been. It also made him think and wonder why Graeme hadn't been in contact or even wanted to meet up. After all, they were brothers and they had a lot to catch up on; he had a lot to tell him about their mam, and for some reason, he felt like he had to apologize to him that she left and started a new life without him. He made a mental note to himself to send another text to Graeme and ask again if they could meet. If he didn't answer, then he would call him or go to his door and see if he would answer it.

Before he knew it he was home and outside of his front door, but he didn't turn the engine off; he just sat there for a while. He wasn't tired as he managed to have some sleep earlier, so he decided what better time than now to go for a drive to Ryhope and see the house that his mam use to live in and the same house that his brother still lived in now. It only took him ten minutes to get there since the roads were empty and all the traffic lights were on the green. It didn't take long at all. He got the address from Devon a few weeks ago, but didn't bother to go and see the house until now while there were no nosy neighbours looking out of their windows wondering who it was driving around in a posh car in this area. Grayson found the house without any problems at all; the streets began with the same letter, which was B, so it was Bevan Avenue and Blyton Avenue. From Devon's text, his brother lived on Bevan Avenue. The house was big and the yard could do with being cleaned up as it looked like it hadn't been done for some time. What Grayson found strange was that it was the early hours of the morning and all the lights were on in the house, so somebody must be home. He stopped himself from getting out of the car and going knocking at the door as it was only five-thirty a.m. and it would be strange at this hour to make a social visit to a brother he didn't know.

Grayson drove away from the house, but he saw in his rear view mirror that somebody, probably his brother, had been looking out of one of the upstairs windows and saw him drive away. Maybe he wouldn't know that it was him as he didn't know what kind of car he drove; he didn't want him to think that he was snooping in on him.

After his driving around for a while, he decided he would go home and rest. He was starting to get hungry so the first thing he would do is make something to eat then sit in front of the television. He had no plans for today and he was back at work that night, so he took it easy as tonight was going to be a long night. Grayson set his alarm on his phone in case he fell asleep so he would wake up in time to have something else to eat and drink, then take a shower before he had to leave for work.

Before Grayson even realized, he was asleep and dreaming. At first, he didn't realize where he was until he recognized the old men that he had been speaking to in the pub, then he looked around and noticed a young lady sitting at the bar who he also recognized, but it couldn't be as he'd found out that she was dead. He noticed that he was watching this play through like he was the third person as he saw himself walk up to the bar and start talking to the young lady, and she started talking to him.

"Hey, my eyes are up here," she'd said, "not down there. That's for later if ya lucky." Then she smiled suggestively. He remembered having this conversation and it was replaying like déjà vu.

Grayson looked up and said, "Sorry, I didn't mean to be rude, but you are beautiful."

She smiled with an even bigger smile. "Thanks, but my name's not beautiful; it's Nikki. What's your name, handsome?"

"Oh, my name's not handsome; it's Grayson. Nice to meet you too, Nikki."

"It's nice to meet you too, Grayson. You're not from around here, are you? I don't remember seeing a good looking lad like you in here before."

Grayson remembered the conversation and a light bulb went off in his head. He realized that she had told him her name and it was Nikki, which she'd had a tattoo of on her wrist. He woke up with a jump and wrote the name down as he would now have to call PC Roberts to let her know that he'd remembered something. He picked up his phone and called PC Roberts on the number that she had given him but, it was constantly busy or went to voicemail. He decided to leave a message and he would try and call again later to make sure she got the message.

"Hi PC Roberts, this is Grayson Taylor Shaw. I just wanted you to know that I remembered something regarding the young lady I was speaking to in the pub. Actually, I had a dream and I remembered some of the conversation I had with her. I don't know if it makes any difference in catching the killer, but she had said that her name was Nikki and it was also tattooed on her wrist. It may not be her real name but at least it's something. I hope this helps, and if you need to speak to me again, then you know how to contact me and where I work so please feel free. Okay, bye."

After finishing the phone call he got up off the couch and went to make himself a coffee and watch television again. It was only three p.m. and he wasn't at work until eight p.m., so he had a few hours to spare. While he had his phone in his hand he decided now would be as good a time as any to send Graeme another message and see if he got any reply back. He decided to write, "Hi Graeme, it's Grayson. I sent you a text a few days back but got no reply. Was just wondering if you fancied meeting up and having a chat. Text me back and let me know when and what time is convenient for you. Hope to hear from you soon." He read through what he wrote and hit the send button and it was gone.

There wasn't much on TV, so he decided to see what had been recorded and decided to watch some Only Fools and Horses which he loved watching. This show always made him laugh especially with Del Boy, Rodney, Grandad and Trigger. The antics they got up to were so funny and Del boy's sayings were funny. Grayson used to use them just to make everyone laugh and to lighten the mood if everyone was having a bad day when he worked in London. He didn't know if they would have the same effect here, but he was going to try at some point. So as Del Boy would say, "He, who dares, wins!"

At 6 p.m. Grayson's alarm went off on his phone and it gave him a shock; he nearly jumped out of his seat as he had forgotten to turn it off when he woke up earlier. He turned the TV off and checked his phone, and he had no messages or missed calls so he put his phone on charge whilst he went to get ready to go in the shower.

By the time he was ready and his phone was fully charged, it was time to go to work. He decided tonight if it wasn't too busy, he would order in pizza for the nurses, doctors, and himself. He was hoping that tonight was going to be a little busier as he was there longer and it would make the night go quicker. Before he went in to start his shift, he noticed that he'd had a voicemail but never heard his phone ring. It was from PC Roberts, so he assumed it was about the message he had sent her earlier in the day.

"Hey, Doctor Shaw, it's PC Natalie Roberts. Thank you for the information you had sent earlier; I'll be sure to pass it on, but that's not the reason I'm calling. I don't know if you are currently at work or at home, but I was just wondering if you'd seen Lauren by any chance. She was supposed to be at work today, but I got a call saying she hadn't shown up. Can you please call me back if you know anything, as this is very important. Thank you and have a nice evening," then the call ended. Grayson found the call strange, as why would PC Roberts be calling asking if he'd seen Lauren? When he'd done his rounds he would go to the Delivery Suite and find out what was going on.

Chapter 18

There had still been no word regarding the disappearance of Lauren, and Natalie was starting to get really worried about her safety. Natalie contacted Lauren's family to see if she had gone there, but she hadn't and her father and brother were on their way to Natalie's to help look for her. Natalie had listened to the voicemail from Doctor Shaw, but it wasn't what she wanted to hear so she passed the information to Detective Stephens about the young lady that had been seen with the doctor and then continued on the search for her love.

It had been over twenty-four hours since she had disappeared and now the whole of CID had been put on the case to search for her partner. A missing person's report had been written and she was hoping that something would come from that. Captain Harris and Special Agent Sharp were a great help, as they went out in the cars to see if they could find her but came back with no answers. They had pulled the CCTV footage from street cameras that were leading to the metro station where it showed Lauren walking with her earphones in listening to music. It also showed her walking into the metro station and down to the platform, but then she disappeared from there and out of sight of any cameras.

She decided at nine p.m. to call Doctor Shaw again as he would be at the hospital on shift and could check in that area if anyone had been brought in fitting her description. She asked Detective Stephens to do the same at the Sunderland Royal Hospital in case she was taken there. When she called Doctor Shaw, he didn't answer straight away so must have been on the ward rounds, and this irritated her as this was now becoming a matter of life and death. When she finally managed to speak to the doctor, he had said that he'd been around the whole hospital and checked records to see if anyone matching her description had been brought in, but there hadn't and it was very unlikely seeing that he was in Newcastle and not Sunderland. He'd gone up to the Delivery Suite but nobody knew anything apart from that she hadn't shown up for work and it worried them as it was very unlike Lauren to miss a shift. Natalie thanked the doctor for checking, and he said once he finished his shift he would come and help search for her. Natalie would take any help she could get to try and find Lauren as she couldn't imagine living her life without her and would do anything for her.

Natalie remembered the first day she had met Lauren; it was when her friend was having a baby. It was Lauren, who was taking care of her friend, and when she entered the delivery room, their eyes met and she hadn't looked away from those eyes since. She had fallen for Lauren hard and would do anything for her. She still felt the same for her as she did the first time she saw her. Lauren wasn't interested in material things and was happy with having just what she needed to get by. She also loved to spend time outdoors and visit new places she had never been before, and Natalie loved to take her places and see the excitement in her eyes. Best thing of all was just spending time together alone and resting in each other's arms, and wishing the days would go slower so that they could spend even more time by themselves.

Lauren loved her job and bringing new life into the world so it really didn't make sense why she wouldn't have gone in. A few of the other midwives had called to ask if there had been any news regarding Lauren's whereabouts, but Natalie couldn't tell them anything new as she didn't have anything to tell. They too had offered their services to come to Sunderland and search for Lauren, but Natalie told them it was okay and she didn't want to run the risk of any of them been caught by the serial killer that was still on the loose.

The last thought had brought tears to Natalie's eyes as she hoped that Lauren hadn't been caught by the serial killer and was now somewhere laying on the edge of the River Wear. Death along the River Wear was the last thing she wanted for the person she hoped to spend the rest of her life with. She had pictured the pair of them growing old together and dying side by side in their bed when the time came. Then they would always be together in life as well as death.

Natalie asked Captain Harris if she could send some patrol officers along the edges of the River Wear just to check that there had been no new bodies placed there, meaning the body of Lauren. Both Captain Harris and Special Agent Sharp agreed that this would be a good idea, and Captain Harris called into the station to have a couple of patrol cars go along both sides to check to see if anything was there.

It then came to Natalie to ask Special Agent Sharp if Lauren would fit in with the profile of this killer and the only thing he could come up with was that if the killer knew that they were searching for him and knew which detectives were on the case, then he could be making a point in taking someone that was close to the lead detective or even trying to make a point to the person he is taking revenge on and show that he can take anyone he wants whether they are close to them or not. Natalie didn't like that answer; in short, the answer was yes, he could have Lauren. He could have already killed her or was even keeping her locked up and torturing her for information that she didn't know. This made Natalie's heart hurt thinking that Lauren has been tortured by this killer, and it also made her angry and even more determined to catch this killer and put him behind bars for the rest of his life.

Half an hour had passed and results from Lauren's phone records had come in but showed nothing unusual apart from a missed call from an unknown number just before she went missing. Natalie didn't know the number and by the looks of the number, it was a burner phone. The number pinged off the cell tower right in the same area of where Lauren had been, so someone must have been watching her and saw that she had earphones in and wouldn't hear anyone approach. The next report to come in was from someone she knew but hadn't seen since she was moved to CID. She saw two uniformed police officers walking towards her from a cruiser. It took her a little time to recognize the person but then she realized who it was. She was happy to see PC Edwards, and he looked as happy to see her but regrettably under the wrong circumstances.

"Hey Natalie, I mean PC Roberts, how are ya doing? Sorry to hear about what's happened. When I heard this job come through, I jumped at the opportunity as you've helped me from day one. If you need anything, partner, then you let me know, okay!"

Natalie forced a smile towards Edwards and nodded her head, "Hey Edwards. Yeah, I'm okay, but I'll be a lot better once I know where Lauren is." Edwards and his new partner nodded their heads understandably.

"Thank you for your help; every little thing helps plus I don't think your partner here appreciates you calling me partner when she's standing right next to you." Edwards's partner was a shy little thing and she reddened when Natalie looked at her.

She put her hand out towards Natalie and said, "Hi, nice to meet ya. I'm sorry about what's happened and I hope we can help. My name is PC Gemma Gray, but everyone just calls me GG for short. Peter, I mean PC Edwards, has spoken so much about you and how much he has learned from you so it's nice to put a face to the name finally." Natalie shook her hand.

Natalie smiled at both of them and she thought GG was a cute little thing and could tell there were sparks of something between both her and Edwards, but she didn't want to say anything as now wasn't the time since both Captain Harris and Special Agent Sharp were close by and could probably hear their conversation.

"Right now I'm just interested in what you guys found along both sides of the river. Did you do the whole length of it? I really need to know as I don't want her to be lying there dying and be all alone."

Peter had to stop Natalie in her tracks and in that frame of thought. "Whoa, whoa there, slow down and stop thinking like that. Four patrol cars, two on both sides, checked every inch along the river and we saw no signs of any bodies or anyone being there recently unless you want to count the wildlife; there was plenty of that but no remains." Edwards took a breath and continued, "GG and I are going to go around the little villages in the area and see if anything stands out on our own time. I'm sure we can get some of the other guys to do the same and we'll report back to you. We won't stop until she is found, okay?" Natalie could feel her eyes starting to water so she had to turn to wipe the tears away, but Peter knew that she was trying to say she was grateful.

Captain Harris came over to check that Natalie was doing okay and asked if she wanted to sit this one out, seeing she was personally linked to the person that had disappeared, and Natalie advised that she didn't and that she was okay to continue. Cynthia updated Natalie that Special Agent Sharp had asked for a repeat test to be done on the DNA that had been found from the previous crime scenes to see if anything new came up. They both expected nothing to come back but it was worth a go just in case it would help find Lauren quicker and maybe even the killer.

Natalie asked Cynthia if it was okay to take the night off so she could update Lauren's family on what was happening and to help search as she felt like she needed to do more to find her. Cynthia advised Natalie that she could and for Natalie to try and get some rest as she wouldn't be of any use to anyone if she was exhausted. Natalie thanked Cynthia and started walking away when she saw Doctor Shaw making his way towards her. For some reason, it gave her a sense of relief to see him there, but she didn't understand why as he was at one point their main suspect but alibis cleared him as he couldn't have been in two places at one time. She knew there was no romantic interest with him but more like a brotherly love since she wasn't interested in men in that kind of way. Cynthia was shocked to see him there; as she didn't think that Natalie knew him personally, but Natalie explained that Lauren worked at the same hospital as Doctor Shaw and that they had worked on a case together for a short time and had become friends. Cynthia accepted this elucidation and gave the go-ahead for him to join the search.

Grayson had finished work early as he wasn't supposed to finish work until the next morning, but he got another doctor to cover for him and said that it was a family emergency and that he was needed as soon as possible. The doctor that covered said it was fine and Grayson left straight away and made his way to the address that Natalie had sent him earlier. He also expected that Natalie hadn't eaten, so he brought them both a sandwich, coffee and water, which would give Natalie time to explain what was going on and what was happening now. Grayson could tell that she was tired and needed rest, but he knew that it would be virtually impossible to get Natalie to rest while Lauren was missing. However, he knew if she didn't, then Natalie would be no use to anyone.

Cynthia caught up with Sharp again and found out what was happening. He advised that if this was a kidnapping, then a ransom call might be made or should have already been made, but if this was the works of the serial killer, then Lauren may already be dead. Cynthia knew this. They would have to wait forty-eight hours for the new DNA results and they had been expedited so that they could get them quicker since everything at this moment was hanging on those results.

Chapter 19

It was five a.m. by the time Grayson got home to get some rest. It was mid-day when he woke up. There still had been no sign of Lauren, and it made him sad for Natalie as he saw how much she loved her. For some reason, Grayson felt a brotherly kinship towards Natalie but he didn't know why, and he wanted to help her so much and bring Lauren home and back to her. Yet he was only a doctor, not a police officer or a Special Agent like the one that he'd seen last night. He looked like everyone else but was sure he could be a badass if the call of duty called for it.

Grayson decided he was going to get up and make some breakfast and a pot of coffee like he usually did and then watch whatever was on television. He called off work for tonight and the following night saying that he was needed for a family emergency still and that he would be back in for the next shift after that. While he waited for the coffee to brew he decided to go to the bathroom. Whilst walking by, he perceived that something had been placed under his front door. He wasn't sure what it was so he walked up to the door and knelt down.

Grayson was perplexed at what he saw. It was a piece of paper with something written on it which was peculiar; why would anyone put something under the door when they could've just knocked and spoken to him personally? He picked the note up and opened it to see what it said; before he started reading, within seconds, he opened the front door and checked both left and right; nobody was there, and how did they manage to get in the front door without a key?

"Hello dear brother, I just wanted you to know that all of this is your fault and that I take great pleasure in telling you that I have your dear friend. I think she said her name was Lauren. I picked her because I saw you talking to her when you were leaving work one day. Remember when you came out that evening and the policewoman was in the reception area, well, so was I. I bet you don't even remember treating me for my wrist, do you? You came in, saw my wrist and then past me on to a nurse. Just so that you know that I'm serious, I left you a little present in front of your door, so please go open your door now."

Grayson had already opened his door and saw a parcel sitting there on the ground. He picked it up and took it into his flat but was careful with it, as he didn't know what was in it but knew he would need to look. He went and got a knife from the kitchen and slowly but steadily opened the box in case it was a bomb. His eyes grew wider with shock with what he found in the box, and it definitely wasn't a bomb. He took a pair of gloves out of his bag that he always carried with him just in case of an emergency and steadily picked up the hand, which, to Grayson, looked like it had just recently been severed from whoever's body it had been taken from. He looked in the box again and saw five teeth which looked like they had been ripped out from the root. He hoped that these weren't Lauren's as, if they were, then she would be in a great deal of pain and by the look of the hand she would be bleeding out.

Grayson placed the hand back in the box, took his gloves off, and went back to the note to continue reading. "As you see brother, I'm very serious in what I say. Poor Lauren here will have a problem trying to deliver babies with one hand, don't you think, and her smile isn't going to be as pretty. Oh, the teeth in the box are from some other victims that I killed because of you, because you took my family away from me. The best part I thought happened nearly a year ago, brother, when I caused our mam to crash and die. See, if I wasn't going to have her in my life then neither were you." Rage rose in Grayson's chest as he finished reading the letter.

Could it actually be that he had purposely made their mam crash her car and die?

The rage got the best of Grayson and he started tossing furniture everywhere. Glass rained down all around him as he threw cups, plates, glass mirrors, tables, chairs; everything he could put his hands on went flying. He sat on the floor when he started to calm down and saw his phone sitting near. He remembered that he would need to call PC Roberts and get her to come to his place immediately as they would really need the box. They would also need to go to

Graeme's house as Lauren may be there and they could get her to safety, as well as Graeme either dead or in a prison cell.

He picked up his phone and dialled Natalie's number; she answered it after the third ring. "Hi Grayson, how are you, and before you ask, no there is still no word about Lauren's whereabouts. I really need to go"

Grayson listened to what Natalie was saying but wasn't really listening, and Natalie noticed when he didn't respond. "Hey, are you okay?"

Grayson eventually answered, "No, I'm not, please come to my place now as I have something for you and some more information. I think I know where Lauren might be."

Grayson could hear Natalie running to her car and hollering to others to follow her as she had a lead. When Natalie got in the car she was still on the phone with Grayson. "Okay, Grayson, we are coming. We'll be there in five minutes so please have the door open."

Grayson assured her that the door would be open and that she should bring a forensic pathologist with them, as what he had to show her wasn't going to be nice. Natalie agreed to bring one and she was getting curious at what Grayson had and what he had to say, but then the phone went dead so Grayson ended the call and decided he needed to try and clean up a little before they got here.

This was going to be hard for both him and Natalie, but he had to do what was right and explain everything to Natalie about his half-brother. He didn't know him, but how could his own brother be the person that has been killing all those poor young ladies and the man that looked like him? Then it made sense to him why the man looked like him as it was his brother's way of trying to kill him. It also made sense regarding the young ladies as they all looked similar to their mother. The light bulb went on in Grayson's head that it had been his brother all along.

As he said he would, he left his main door and his front door to his apartment open so that the police and Natalie could walk straight in without having to wait. Five minutes had passed but they still weren't there so he took the opportunity to go and put a pair of jeans and a t-shirt on. When he came back out of his room he heard the pounding of feet coming towards his apartment, then the door burst open and Natalie was the first one across the threshold. Behind her were Captain Harris, Detective Stephens, Special Agent Sharp and some other cops in uniform. They all looked around and noticed that something had happened as the place was still askew with books, glass, seats, and tables still lying around and out of place. They looked at Grayson in a way that asked what had happened and all he said with a shrug of the shoulders was "temper," and they just nodded their heads.

The problem for Grayson was where to start, but before he got the chance Captain Harris got a phone call and she excused herself and went out to the hallway. Grayson straightened the furniture, brushed off the broken glass and made room for everyone to sit. Natalie noticed the box that was sitting on the kitchen counter where Grayson had moved it and she couldn't take her eyes off it. Grayson noticed and advised Natalie that they would soon get to that as time was of the essence. He asked if they should wait for the Captain and they answered that it was probably a good idea as she should hear everything he had to say.

Grayson asked Natalie to sit down as he had a question to ask her "PC Roberts, I don't know what it is about you, but I feel like we're connected in some way. I just don't know how, but every time I see you, I want to protect you. Can I ask a personal question?"

Natalie looked around and hoped that Cynthia wasn't going to be long then she turned to Grayson and replied, "You know what, I felt the same when I saw you when you came yesterday to search for Lauren. When I saw you I felt relief and didn't understand why. Yeah, go ahead ask your question."

Grayson looked her straight in the eyes.

"May I ask what your mother's name is or was?"

Natalie nodded. "Yeah sure, my mother's name is Margot Roberts."

Grayson thought about what she said and the name Margot sounded familiar then he asked, "Do you know what her maiden name was?"

Natalie replied, "Her maiden name was Self, why?"

With this Grayson smiled back at Natalie as now it made sense why it felt like he had to protect her and be there for her. "Well, I guess now everything makes sense."

Natalie was confused with what he had just said and now wanted answers. "What makes sense now? What is this about?"

Grayson put his hand out to calm Natalie down. "Can you remember a week or so ago, your mother going to meet a nephew that she never knew existed with her brother and sisters?"

Natalie barely remembered her mother mentioning something about it, but she never really paid much attention as she was busy with this case. "Yeah, I remember her saying she was going to the Oak Tree Farm pub to meet a nephew that they never knew anything about. How do you know that?"

He smiled at Natalie and replied, "I'm the nephew she was going to meet at the Oak Tree Farm pub and I'm the one they never knew existed. I'm your long-lost cousin, Natalie."

The surprise on Natalie's face spoke a thousand words and Grayson could see that she was playing the conversation over in her head when she spoke.

"Now I know what you mean." Grayson didn't understand what she meant.

"What do you mean?"

Natalie looked at Grayson and replied, "Now everything makes sense. Why I feel this connection to you. Can I ask who your mother is?"

Grayson put his head down "Was. My mother was Tracey, the one that left and went to London."

As she was nodding her head, Grayson saw that the realization was hitting her and she said, "WOW! Do you know that you have a brother?" Grayson knew the next part was going to be hard for Natalie as it meant that the serial killer was her own cousin Graeme. Grayson started scratching his head as he knew it was time to come clean and tell Natalie everything that had happened.

"Yeah, I know about Graeme and I have something to tell you, but I have to start from the beginning."

Just when he was about to start, Captain Harris came bursting back into the apartment. "Okay, we have a possible match from the DNA and the remarkable thing is that it's a familial match to you, Grayson." He knew exactly what she meant, and he asked Captain Harris to sit while he told them what had happened. This was a long story to tell and there was no time like the present, so he started from the beginning; all eyes were on him.

Chapter 20

The astounding things that Grayson was telling Natalie and the others were beyond mind-blowing. He had started from the very beginning. He had enlightened them about the car crash his mother had died in and then his search for his mother's side of the family that he knew nothing about. He also said about quitting his big job in a London hospital so that he could move up north to find and get to know his family. He then went on to tell them about finding out from their cousin Devon that he had a half-brother who was only three years older than him. Grayson said that he had tried texting and calling to try and get Graeme to meet him, but he would never call back. He also said about meeting the young lady called Nikki in the pub, and though she was very beautiful, he wasn't into doing one night stands. He had left money behind the bar for her to get a couple of drinks and gave her some money for a taxi at the end of the night, but he had left alone after that. The next morning on television he had found out that Nikki had been murdered and then he called and came to the station to make a statement so that he wasn't hiding anything. He would have looked more like a suspect if he hadn't mentioned anything.

Captain Harris, Detective Stephens, and Natalie looked at each other as from day one they had suspected Grayson of being the killer, but after the alibis had cleared him of any wrongdoing, they had nothing to hold him on. Grayson decided now would be a good time for everyone, including Special Agent Sharp, to have a drink as it was only going to get more interesting from now on. He offered them all coffee, tea, water or diet coke, and put a few snacks on a plate in case anyone was hungry then sat back down when he remembered it would be time to bring the box and letter over and invite the forensic pathologist in as the box would need to leave for DNA and prints to be taken. It was too late to try and reconnect the hand as the tissue would have already died.

When Grayson was comfortable back in his chair he started with this morning's events. He told them all what had happened and gave Natalie the letter first that had been slipped under his door at some point that morning. Natalie was taken aback by what she was reading, then she handed the letter to the Captain and she passed it on until everyone had read it. After reading the letter Natalie stood up and went to the box and was about to open it until Grayson warned her that what was in the box would be shocking. Special Agent Sharp advised that everyone should quickly look and whatever was in would need to be taken away so that any evidence that was there could be caught and filed.

After looking in the box Natalie felt like she was going to be sick since the hand in the box could well be Lauren's. She was ready to jump up and leave to go to Graeme's house. Captain Harris and Special Agent Sharp stopped her as they had to be careful on how to approach the house in case he had cameras to spot them if they ever came. Grayson felt partly guilty as it was his brother that had done all this, but at the same time he didn't really know Graeme and hoped he would get everything that he deserved.

By the time Grayson had finished telling them everything, everyone was on their feet and ready to leave. Before they left he offered them a suggestion and basically made himself bait to get Graeme away from Lauren if she was in the house. As Graeme had said it was his fault that Lauren had been captured and he was the one that he wanted revenge on.

Natalie didn't like the idea of Grayson making himself bait, but she thought it was a good idea and so did everyone else. Natalie realized that that's how Lauren had been taken as easily, as she knew who Graeme was, and he must have known where all the cameras were in the metro station and knew how to steer away from them to stay out of sight. Lauren knew how to protect herself as Natalie had taught her self-defence, so he must have used something else to get her to go with him.

Natalie asked if there was anything else they should know and Grayson shook his head, because as far as he knew that was everything. Captain Harris told Grayson to grab his things as he was going along with them, but if things were to change, then he had to stand aside and let them do their job. Grayson agreed with the terms, but he knew he would do anything to get Lauren back even if that cost him his own life.

Captain Harris was on the phone the majority of the time organizing patrol cars to do drives around the area of the house and to check to see if there was any movement in the house. She also called in a Tactical Aide Unit to help with the takedown of the suspect once he was in reach, as they were specialists in the takedown of a suspect once they were in this kind of situation. Word had come back from the patrol units that a car was in the driveway and there was movement from within, so Captain Harris gave everyone the go ahead and advised Grayson to be ready to do his part.

When they arrived in Ryhope, they stopped their cars down the street from the house so as not to give away that they were making their way to the house. What nosy neighbours came out to see what was going on were told to go back inside and stay away for their own safety in case Graeme now had a gun.

Natalie was starting to get nervous as she had the possibility of getting Lauren back but at the same time quite possibly lose a cousin she had just found. She made sure that Grayson was ready and prepared and put a Taser gun in his pocket, as the first chance he got he would have to use it to bring down his brother. Grayson knew what he had to do and was mentally preparing himself for the task ahead. He thought to himself that this was nothing like being prepared for a big surgery but also thought to himself that he could be saving a life, which was all he was about. And in this case it was Lauren's life he was saving.

Captain Harris asked Natalie if everything was in order and if everyone was in their places so that she could give her go-ahead to start the takedown. What she was actually meaning was, was Grayson ready to walk up to the front door to confront his brother so that the tactical unit could go in via the back door? Natalie looked at Grayson and asked him again if he was ready. He nodded his head and opened the car door to get out. Natalie advised him that he didn't have to do it, but Grayson insisted that he did.

Special Agent Sharp was standing outside the car door and walked Grayson through some things to do and not to do. Grayson had to give Graeme the illusion that he was in control and to keep him talking so that the tactical unit could penetrate the back door without Graeme even noticing. Grayson nodded and confirmed to Sharp that he knew what he had to do. Natalie gave Grayson a hug and put an ear bug listening device in his ear so they could hear everything that was said; if he got into trouble, then they would know when to run in.

Grayson took one last look at everyone standing around; that made him a little nervous, if not petrified, as he'd never done anything like this before. Now he knew why he never wanted to be in the police force. He calmed his nerves and started what had seemed like a very long walk towards Graeme's front door. He could hear in his ear Captain Harris telling the tactical unit to be ready as the bait was on the hook. Grayson found this funny as he'd never thought of himself as bait for fish before, so he had a little laugh at himself and was just reaching the gate to walk up to his brother's door. To him, it felt like he was walking to be executed on death row, but all in all, he had to do it. Natalie felt like she had to pull Grayson out of this and not risk his life, but he wanted to do it so she kept quiet and listened to Grayson's rapid breathing through the earpiece she had put in his ear.

Next, she heard him declare.

"Okay, I'm here and about to knock on the door. Be ready." The next thing Natalie heard was three loud bangs as Grayson knocked on Graeme's front door. She wanted to run up and get Lauren out of there, but if she did, then she knew she would blow the whole operation and risk both Lauren and Grayson's lives.

Chapter 21

There was no sound coming from the house after Grayson's first knocks, so he raised his hand and banged on the door three more times a little louder than the first time. He could hear someone moving around and then he heard a voice.

"Who is it and what diya want? If ya selling summit, then I dinnit want anything."

Grayson thought about his words carefully before he answered. "Hey Graeme, it's Grayson. Can you come and open the door, please? I got your note this morning and I wanted to look the person in the face who sent me it."

Grayson heard a voice in his ear and it was Special Agent Sharp, "Be careful what you say as he may back away and not answer."

As he heard this, he sighed and said, "Okay, okay."

"Why should I open the door?" he heard Graeme say.

He thought about what he had to say next, then said, "Graeme, come on, open the door so I can meet my brother. I want to talk to you seeing as you won't reply to any of my calls or texts."

"Is anyone with ya, like the pigs?" Grayson knew that the nickname for the police in the north was the pigs.

"No, there are no pigs with me; it's just me. I won't come in if you don't want me to, but at least open the door and talk to me." Grayson heard nothing but silence after this as if Graeme was considering it.

"Come on, Graeme. I need to apologize to you for a lot of things and I want to say them to your face, otherwise it means nothing." This time he heard somebody, probably Graeme, walk up to the front door.

"Yeah, ya do need to apologize for a lot. Ya took my family away from me and now I have neebody. All because of you, ya fucking bastard."

Grayson shook his head as it was Graeme who killed their mam by causing her accident.

"Graeme, did you know that mam was planning on coming up to see the family at some point before you killed her?"

He knew this would get a reaction out of Graeme, "No, she wasn't, you're a liar. How would you know that?" Then the door swung open and Grayson was face to face with his half-brother. He looked so much like their mam, and it made him take a step back.

Captain Harris and the others saw this opportunity to go in now while Grayson had his attention. "Tactical Unit, move now. The suspect is at front door," she ordered.

The order was heard through Grayson's earpiece, and he tried to keep Graeme's attention while they were making their move.

"Yeah, I was told a couple of weeks ago that she was planning on coming up to make amends with the family. She would have been coming to see you, but you took that opportunity away by causing the crash."

This made Graeme think, but then his features changed and he replied, "Well instead of dying in a car crash, she would have died from my bare hands dear brother, as I still wouldn't have forgiven her for abandoning me."

Orders were starting to come through his earpiece and it was distracting Grayson a little from his train of thought, Graeme picked up on it and started to back away.

Grayson asked, "Can I ask why you killed all those young people?"

Graeme smirked at Grayson and answered, "Aye, of course ya can ask, and the answer is that they reminded me of our mam, I wanted to kill her over and over again."

Another question came to mind, but first, he asked, "Instead of standing here can we go inside as it looks like it's going to start raining…"

Graeme looked up into the sky. "Nah, it looks fine to me and no, ya cannit come inside as ya not welcome, ya cockney fucker. We may have the same blood because of our mam but ya, not my brother. Do you want to know why I killed those two blokes?"

Grayson knew the answer but he asked anyway, "Why?"

He replied, "I killed them because they reminded me of you and I want ya dead."

That was what Grayson thought and just nodded his head. He heard through his earpiece that the tactical unit had gained entry and was now making their way through the house, so he knew he would have to keep Graeme talking so that he didn't turn around and go back inside. Grayson deliberated to himself if this was what negotiators did when they went to save people that were being held captive, as he was starting to feel like one.

"Okay, Graeme, if you wanted to kill me so bad, then why didn't you just do it from the beginning and not kill all those young ladies and those two men? They didn't do anything to you."

A smile came across Graeme's face as he already knew his answer, "What would have been the fun in that, dear brother? You should have stayed in London and never came here."

Rage was starting to rise again in Grayson and he could feel the Taser gun in his pocket; he was waiting for the right opportunity to use it, but he wanted to get the entire story out of Graeme because otherwise he would never know the whole explanation.

"You are the lucky one, Graeme, not me. At least you knew who your family was, I didn't. I had to find out after you killed our mam and that's why I had to come and move here to find out who they were. You have grown up with cousins, aunties, and uncles all of your life, while mine has been filled with secrecy."

This made Graeme think, as he had known all of his family even though he didn't have anything to do with them; his father was to blame for that as he didn't want him anywhere near his mother's relatives.

Graeme couldn't think of anything to say to this so he just answered with, "Ah well, it's a bit late now, isn't it? What's done is done and I enjoyed every minute of it. Do you think I'll get a nickname like the Wear Strangler or something like that?"

Grayson didn't want to answer that question as the Special Agent had told him not to feed his ego. Instead he asked, "Can I ask you, Graeme, do you have Lauren?"

Again a smile came across Graeme's face as he was about to answer. "Ah Lauren, yes, I do have Lauren. You would have thought that it would've been harder to take her, but as soon as I said that our cousin Natalie wanted to see her at my house, she came without question, which on her behalf was a bit stupid, don't ya think?"

It was time for Grayson to ask the question as to whether Lauren was still alive, and he knew that Natalie was listening through the earpiece in his ear, "Just out of curiosity, is Lauren still alive? I was just wondering as that will be another body to blame me for."

With this Graeme started laughing, and that angered Grayson even more, but he knew he had to get the answer. "Well dear brother, yes, she is still alive, but only just as she lost a lot of blood when I took her hand and then her bottom tooth. Why do you care anyway? You know she's a lesbian, right? And that's she's Natalie partner?"

Grayson replied, "Yes, I do care, because I care about all life, even yours, and yes, I do know that she's Natalie's partner. One last question before I leave, Graeme..."

"Yeah, what question is that, brother?" Graeme asked.

"What did you use to kill all those other people?" Grayson looked at his brother with a questioning look.

"Oh that question..., Well, I used my own garrote that I made. Did you know that there are videos on YouTube that show you how to make them? It's very interesting; you should check it out."

In his earpiece, he heard the order to take him down with the Taser gun from Natalie, but Grayson wasn't finished but was aware of everything going on around him.

"I don't think I will as I'm about saving lives, Graeme not taking them." He was about to bring out the Taser gun in his pocket to use when he saw movement behind him but tried to not let Graeme notice that he saw it. "You're right about one thing though, Graeme; we are not brothers but only have the same bloodline. We are nothing alike."

Just at that moment, Grayson pulled out the Taser gun to shoot Graeme with an electric charge, but he didn't realize at the same time that Graeme had something in his hand and brought it round at the same time. He took the shot, but he had a gun. Grayson felt a pain run through his shoulder and then felt himself dropping to the floor at the same time he shot Graeme with the Taser gun and he went down too. He didn't see anything in Graeme's hand, so where did the gun come from? At the same time, he heard Graeme say, "I bet you didn't know I had that, did ya? Now die, ya bastard, along with our mam."

Before Grayson lost consciousness he heard screams and shouts coming from his earpiece. He couldn't tell if it was Natalie or Captain Harris, but it was someone saying that he'd been shot. Next, he saw lots of people running to secure Graeme and put him in handcuffs to lead him away, but he remembered hearing him laughing.

Natalie came rushing up to Grayson and tried to stop the blood coming from his shoulder, but then she quickly left as the paramedics came to help. Natalie ran into the house as she searched for Lauren. Grayson was drifting more and more into unconsciousness. The last thing he remembered hearing was Natalie shouting Lauren's name and feet running from room to room then up and down stairs until everything went silent and the darkness claimed Grayson.

Chapter 22

It had been a few days since Grayson had been shot and he had been unconscious for that whole time. He had been operated on three times due to complications from the gunshot to his chest next to his shoulder. When he eventually awoke he saw someone asleep in the chair next to him but didn't know who it was. He really needed a drink of water and tried to get their attention. As he became more aware of his surroundings, he realized he was in a hospital bed and the pain began to get increasingly worse; then he remembered he had been shot by his own brother.

"It's about time you woke up, sleepy head," he heard someone say then he realized that it was Natalie that was awake and sitting next to him.

"You had me worried for a moment as we thought you'd never wake up." He noticed that she said 'we' and he wondered who else was there, but before that he really needed a drink.

"Water, I need a drink of water," he said with a raspy voice. Natalie got up and got the pitcher of water that was at the side of Grayson. She poured it into a glass that had a straw in it and offered the water to him while holding on to the glass so that it didn't spill all over him. He was grateful for the drink and then tried to move, but he realized it sent a shooting pain all the way down his right side.

Natalie realized what he was trying to do and tried to stop him, "Don't move, Grayson. You're going to open the wound up if you try to move. Just stay still and I'll call for the nurse to come and help you."

After the nurse and doctors had been in to see him and moved him to a sitting position, he finally got the strength to ask Natalie questions and find out where he was and what had happened after he passed out. "Well, a lot has happened while you've been sleeping. Firstly, you're at the Sunderland Royal Hospital, but they thought that they were going to have to transfer you to the RVI as they couldn't stop the internal bleeding from the bullet wound. Then after the third operation, they managed to stop the bleeding and you started to improve, so they called off the transfer and just got you comfortable here in your own private room."

"When I woke up, you said *we* were worried. Who are *we*?" Grayson asked.

Natalie smiled. "Oh yeah, I did didn't I? You have a whole fan club of people out in the waiting area hoping to see you and give you their well wishes. Do you want me to go and get them?"

There was no way he wanted a whole lot of people in, so he asked, "Who is out there?"

Natalie smiled, but she could tell that Grayson's strength was wearing down quickly and that he didn't really want anyone in. "Well, there's my Captain, Special Agent Sharp, Detective Stephens, some of the Tactical Unit, some of your relatives, your dad, and a special someone who wants to come and see you."

Grayson didn't know who that could be so he made fun of it. "I'm not really up to seeing anyone right now, as I'm starting to feel tired again, so maybe later. The special someone shouldn't be allowed in here as you're not supposed to get booty calls in the hospital." They both started to laugh but Grayson realized it hurt too much to laugh.

Still laughing, Natalie liked the fact he was trying to make light of the subject but then replied, "No, no, not that kind of special someone. Can I please go, get the person and bring them in before you fall asleep again?"

Smiling back at Natalie he said, "Yeah sure, go and get whoever it is and give my apologies to everyone else. Maybe I'll get to see them tomorrow after I've had a good night's rest."

Natalie got up out of the chair she had earlier fallen asleep in and went to pass on the message to everyone and get the person she was going to take in. Everyone understood and was just glad that he was doing okay; they told Natalie to let Grayson know that they would be back another time to check on him.

After Natalie had told the special person that he would see them, they made their way back to his room. As they entered the room, Grayson's eyes were shut. Natalie wondered if he was more tired than he had said and had fallen asleep, until he opened his eyes and a small smile brightened his face. Before he could say anything, Lauren wrapped her arms around Grayson, but the pain in his chest and shoulder made him grimace with pain so Lauren let go and sat down in the seat that Natalie had been sitting in earlier. They both went to speak at the same time then stopped and laughed.

Grayson told Lauren to go first so she did, and he could see tears building in her eyes as she started to speak. "I don't know in how many words I can say this but thank you for saving my life. If you hadn't come and distracted the crazy ass monster, then I think I would be dead right now."

Grayson nodded and replied to what Lauren had just said, "You don't need to thank me, Lauren; you need to be thanking your girlfriend here who put it all together. I was just the bait to get Graeme away from you, and I got a bullet in my shoulder for my efforts." Lauren wanted to ask how he was, but she could see how he was feeling so didn't bother to ask.

He noticed that there was something different about Lauren; her hair was a different colour. The last time he saw her, her hair was a light brown but now it was blonde. He was just about to ask Lauren if she'd coloured her hair blonde, but then he remembered that Graeme must have done it to make her look more like his mam so that it would be easier to kill her while thinking that Lauren was their mam.

He decided not to ask Lauren about it as it might bring up bad memories for her, but Lauren noticed that Grayson was looking at her hair and she said, "Yeah, he dyed my hair. He knocked me out when I got to the house, and when I woke up my hair was blonde and, my left hand and one of my teeth were missing."

Grayson shook his head. "I'm sorry for what he did to you."

Lauren shook her head and took a hold of his hand "You have nothing to be sorry for. It wasn't you and anyways, you saved my life. Natalie told me that you figured out that she is actually your cousin. I was surprised when she told me, so that means that Graeme was related to both of you."

Grayson raised his head. "Yeah, isn't that a weird set of circumstances?" He looked at Natalie at this point and asked, "Speaking of my brother, where is he and what's happening?"

Natalie looked at Grayson then replied, "He's in jail awaiting sentencing. He has been charged with all the murders along the River Wear and the attempted murder of you and Lauren. Also the assault on the other lady who we got to identify Graeme as the person who attacked her."

Grayson nodded his head in agreement as he was happy with what he had just heard. His eyes started to close as he could feel the need for sleep surround him, so Natalie and Lauren said their goodbyes and each said thank you.

Before they even got to leave the room, Grayson was already asleep. He had pressed the morphine IV to give himself another dose so that he couldn't feel the pain as much. Natalie would be forever grateful to Grayson for putting his life at risk to save the woman she loved.

As she walked Lauren back to her own room, she caught sight of Grayson's dad and told him that he was welcome to go in and sit with his son while he slept. Patrick nodded his head, picked up his things, and made his way to Grayson's room. He tried to be quiet when he opened the door as not to wake his son, who needed all the rest that he could get. Seeing his son this way brought tears to his eyes, but wiped those away before anyone saw a grown man cry.

Lauren was going to be in the hospital for a little while longer due to the extensive damage that had been caused when Graeme had taken her hand, but Natalie would be here every day to see her, and Lauren's family were with her too.

Natalie had to go to work the next day to close up the case and finalize everything for the case against her own cousin. Captain Harris had been there every step of the way with Natalie, and she would have to thank her and also Detective Stephens and Special Agent Sharp, who helped with his profile.

Chapter 23

It had been early morning when Natalie got into the station with coffee in hand. Not many people were in work yet, but she saw that Captain Harris and Special Agent Sharp were in the Captain's office talking and drinking coffee, so she went and knocked on the door to say hello.

Both Cynthia and Andy smiled when Natalie opened the door, and they waved her in to join them. Cynthia looked at the time then at Natalie. "Why are you in so early, Natalie? It's only seven-thirty a.m. and you have three hours before the files are needed."

She shrugged her shoulders at Cynthia and replied, "Just thought I would go over the files one more time and make sure we have everything to convict. I don't want any chance of Graeme getting off with a technicality, and I want to make sure he's put away for life so nobody else gets hurt."

They both nodded their heads with understanding, and then Andy offered his services to Natalie to help and make sure everything was in order. Natalie took him up on his offer and they left Cynthia's office together, whilst she continued making phone calls. Natalie and Andy entered the conference room. Natalie noticed that Andy was quiet and she didn't understand why, so she asked, "Are you okay, Andy? It looks like you have something on your mind."

Andy shook this off and replied, "No, no, I'm good. I'm just thinking about a case at home that I have to go back to. One of our agents has been kidnapped and no ransom has been asked for yet."

Now Natalie understood what was on his mind, "I'm sorry. When do you leave here to go back to the other side of the pond?"

Whilst gathering the paperwork and marking the file, Andy answered, "I actually have to leave in an hour for my connecting flight to France."

Natalie nodded, "Ah okay, that's fast. Okay well, I'll take you to the hotel to pick your things up, then I'll take you to the airport if you like."

Andy smiled. "Yeah, that would be awesome, thank you, but first I want to speak to you about something." Natalie had an inquisitive look on her face as she didn't know what he was about to say.

Andy looked at Natalie and he could see that she didn't know what he was going to say, so he comforted her with, "Its okay, Natalie, don't worry. It's nothing bad or about the case, relax."

Andy smiled and this took the pressure off Natalie's shoulders.

Andy continued, "I have been speaking with Captain Harris and my team about your work with this case and we would like to offer you an open invitation to come to America and work with my team and get specialized training in our field. If after that you want to come home, then so be it, but if you and Lauren want to stay and build a life for yourselves there, then we will help you with that. There is no expiry date on this offer, so feel free to take your time and talk it through with Lauren." Andy gave Natalie his business card. "This is my card, so feel free to contact me at any time. My personal cell number and home number are on the back if I'm not at the office. My team is already hoping that you will return with me, but I told them that you want to see this case through and close it with a conviction, and they understand that."

This left Natalie thunderstruck as she'd only just moved up to CID, and now she had been given an opportunity to move to America with Lauren. She thought she was dreaming so she pinched herself hard on the arm to check, and she realized it wasn't a dream, but reality. Then she thought that they were pulling a prank on her, but then nobody else was in the office so it couldn't have been a prank.

She looked into Andy's eyes then asked, "Are you serious? You want me to come to America and train and work with you and your team?"

Andy nodded, "Yep, that is definitely what I'm implying, but now it's in your hands if you're up for the challenge."

Natalie smiled. "I'm definitely up for the challenge, but as you referred to earlier, I want to see this case through to the end and make sure Graeme gets the sentence that he deserves. Also, Lauren is going to have a lot of hospital visits regarding her amputation and I want to be here for that."

Understandably Andy knew exactly what she was talking about. He said, "I actually have something else for you. I have been up all night, and if or when you decide to come, Lauren will get help with her amputation and everything else, all expenses paid by your Captain. That also includes dental work for the missing tooth too."

Natalie was in reverence of what she just heard. The Captain was going to pay to help Lauren; wow, she couldn't believe it. A hundred things were now rushing through Natalie's head. It was then the correct procedure for saying thank you but she didn't care. She grabbed a hold of Special Agent Sharp and hugged him.

She could feel tears coming to her eyes, but she didn't want to cry so she bit her lip and stepped away and turned before he could see that her eyes were wet. "WOW! Thank you so much. This is an amazing offer and I will definitely talk to Lauren about it when I go to see her this afternoon. I can't promise that we will take your offer, but we will definitely consider it. Again, thank you."

Andy nodded and beamed. "No need to thank me, Natalie. You have earned this opportunity. Stay here for a couple of months if need be and learn more from the Captain, but she is fully aware of my offer to you and she is willing to let you take advantage in as early as six months' time, you will also be staying on with CID unless something comes up and I need you there earlier."

"Ah right, okay, that seems a bit quick but I'm up for it, and as I said I'll speak to Lauren and see what she says." By this time Natalie was smiling from ear to ear and they hadn't realized the time.

Andy said, "Okay, well think about it, but right now we need to make a move if I'm going to check in on time for my connecting flight." Natalie looked at the time, made a move towards the conference room door and kept it open for Andy as he walked past. She saw Cynthia watching them as they left and she waved goodbye to Special Agent Sharp. Then Natalie mouthed 'thank you' to her and Cynthia nodded in acceptance.

They made it to Newcastle International Airport with time to spare and Andy checked in for his flight. Just before he turned to go to departures he said, "Okay, well I better get going and until I see you again, Natalie Roberts this is not goodbye but see you soon on my side of the pond."

Natalie smiled and said as Andy was going up the escalator, "See you soon, Andy Sharp" and then he was gone.

Everything regarding the case files was in order thanks to the help of Special Agent Sharp, who would now be in France, so Natalie decided she was finished for the day and she was going to go to the hospital to see Lauren. She had a lot to talk to Lauren about and Natalie was hoping that she would be as excited as she was about the invitation offered by Special Agent Sharp.

By the time Natalie got to the hospital, it was twelve forty-five p.m. and visiting hours were due to finish in fifteen minutes, but she was hoping that the nurses would give her time to stay and explain everything properly to Lauren. When she got to Lauren's room she was just lying on the bed watching television and Natalie just stood there for a moment to look at her and she thought she looked like an angel. When Lauren saw Natalie standing at the door she smiled, as it seemed like forever since the last time she had seen Natalie.

"Hey, baby, you're early. I wasn't expecting to see you until later," Lauren said.

Natalie beamed, "I can leave and come back later if you want."

Lauren shook her head. "No, no, come here and give me a hug and tell me what you've been up to this morning."

Natalie went over to Lauren and gave her a kiss and a hug then said, "Well, this morning I've just been making sure that the case file is complete and took Special Agent Sharp to the airport so that he could catch his flight back to France then America." Lauren smiled and Natalie continued, "Oh, and while I remember, Special Agent Sharp offered me a chance to go and work with his team in America and for you to come along. All treatment that you'll have over there is paid for by Captain Harris, that's all."

Lauren couldn't believe what she just heard and the look on her face spoke more than a thousand words. "Does that mean we're going to America?"

Natalie smiled, "Yes baby, we're going to America in no less than six months. Are you okay with that?"

She couldn't believe it and Lauren answered, "Sign me up, baby. Let's get out of here; America here we come."

Chapter 24

Two weeks after the initial shooting, it was time for Grayson to go home to his flat and finish his recovery. He was given a few weeks of painkillers, antibiotics, and a few weeks of physiotherapy to get full movement back in his shoulder, which he couldn't wait for so he could get back to work. He had also been ordered by Captain Harris to see a psychiatrist so that he could talk through his feelings and also in case there were any signs of Post-Traumatic Stress Disorder (PTSD). All the sitting in his flat would send him crazy and he could only take so much daytime TV. Lauren and Natalie had offered him a place to stay with them, but he politely declined the offer as he didn't want to invade their space and, to be truthful, he wanted his own space too.

Grayson's dad had stayed in the area and wanted his son to stay with him, because he was honestly now scared for his son's life in this area. Again Grayson turned him down and told his dad that he already had a flat and would remain there for the near future until he decided if he was going to move closer to his mam's side of the family in the little old coal mining village of Ryhope where he was ironically shot by his own brother.

After a very restless night of sleep, Grayson decided he was going to go for a walk around town as he needed to get a few things in, especially food as the food that he had was now stale or had grown a pair of legs and was starting to walk on its own. To make things easier on himself, he decided that some quick microwave meals would be easier for him to make until his shoulder healed a little more and had more range in it to be able to make something better. Some ready-made food was also going to be on his list and some fruit juices, coffee, his good old faithful Pringles, and maybe even a couple of bags of Maltesers.

Someone must have come in and cleaned the flat because if he remembered correctly, when he left the flat the last time, he had destroyed a lot of his furniture when he lost his temper. Now everything was back together or had been replaced with the same identical piece of furniture, so you would never have thought that anything had happened. If his landlord had seen the mess he had left, then he would have been majorly pissed, so whoever cleaned up saved him a major headache.

Natalie had mentioned to him the other day that the special agent from America had given her the opportunity to go and work across the pond as he was very impressed with the work that she had done on this case. She would learn more over there regarding serial killers, kidnappers, and terrorists and so on, which she sounded very excited about as you could tell it in her eyes and voice. Natalie had also mentioned that Lauren was offered help regarding her injuries, which was amazing news and Lauren was very excited too. He had only just found this cousin and now she was going to take off to

America. She mentioned it wasn't going to be for a good few months yet so there was plenty of time, and he could always go over for a holiday and meet up with them.

Captain Harris had come to see Grayson just before he left the hospital and asked if he would be a witness against his brother at his trial, which was to start in the next couple of weeks. She said if he didn't want to, it was okay, but he would be able to put the final nail in his brother's coffin for a sure conviction. Grayson said it would be his pleasure to hammer that nail in once and for all as Graeme was also getting charged with attempted murder for shooting him. He had no feelings for his so-called brother, so the pleasure would be all his.

Devon and the rest of his mam's side of the family came to see him when he was in the hospital and they were in utter shock at what had been happening right under their noses. They felt ashamed that one of their own family members could do something as heinous as this, but they were happy that both Lauren and Grayson had survived. Devon's mam, Kate, had suggested when both of them were feeling better that they could maybe have another family get together and get to know Grayson a bit better, especially if he was planning on staying around for a while. Grayson responded saying he would love that and maybe his dad would also join them, if that was okay with them. They loved the idea and would love to meet the man Tracey eventually married and made a life with.

It was starting to get late and Grayson noticed that the pain was starting to get worse, so he took his medication and decided it was time for bed. He changed the gauze on his wounds which hurt like hell, but he got it done. He hoped he didn't have the same nightmare as he did the night before which was Graeme standing in front of him with a gun pointed at his head and firing it and then he was dead. That's when he woke in cold sweats and couldn't get back to sleep in fear of having the same nightmare again. He would finally get too tired and would pass out, too tired to even dream. Grayson would tell himself that tomorrow was just another day, and he would eventually get back to work.

Chapter 25

The next morning was rough for Grayson because he felt nothing but excruciating pain from his shoulder; it made him wonder if he needed to go back to the hospital for them to check it out. He took the dressing from the wound, which looked very red but had no sign of any infection. Grayson decided he would just clean the area and redress it with a fresh dressing, then take his painkillers and the antibiotics for now. He started to wish he still had the morphine that he had in the hospital.

Grayson was about to take his pills when he just happened to glance at the floor next to his front door and realized that there was a letter lying on the ground. This brought back some bad memories for him, and he couldn't decide whether to pick it up and open it or pick it up and throw it straight in the bin without reading it.

He took his pills, all the time wondering what the letter could be. He didn't notice until he wiped his head that he was starting to sweat and also that he was shaking. Whether it was from being worried or from the pain now coming from his arm, he didn't know. He built up the courage and walked over to the door then stared at the letter on the floor.

He felt like he had been staring at it for a while, yet only five minutes had passed. He bit the bullet and picked the letter up but didn't open it. He turned it over in his hands a few times and noticed that it looked harmless; maybe it was from his landlord or Natalie, but surely they would have knocked on the door if it was from them.

Grayson chuckled at himself for been so apprehensive about a letter, but the recent past had proved you never know what could be inside the envelope and from whom. It had been long enough, so he made the decision to open the letter and find out who it was from. He read the first two lines and wished he had just thrown it away, but now that he started he may as well finish it.

"I knew you were trouble when you came here, you cockney fucking wanker. You should've stayed where you belonged, or even better, you should have died when I put a bullet in you.

You think these bars are going to hold me forever you asshole. I'll get you and that bitch one way or the other, and I'll kill all of you. If I die in here, then I'm gonna haunt the lot of you for making my life a living hell.

One thing that I'm sure you haven't thought of, dickhead, is how did I get this letter to you if I'm locked up? I have a secret that you don't know about and by the time you figure it out, then either Natalie, Lauren, or yourself will be dead. I'm going to enjoy every second of knowing how you died, including every little detail, down to how the life of you drained from your eyes. I'm not only going to enjoy the fact of your suffering, but also the fact that you will no longer be on the face of this earth.

I know about the offer that our sweet dyke cousin, Natalie, has been given about going to America, but I have my own way of making that interesting for everyone. It's not going to be plain sailing, especially if I have anything to do with it. Don't worry, dear brother, I have also sent a sweet letter to my cousin similar to this one, so no need to call her as I'm sure you will hear from her very soon.

Well, that's all for now and sorry I didn't send you any presents this time, but you never know, some might turn up, so keep an eye out and always keep looking behind you as I promise you this... I WILL KILL YOU one way or another."

Grayson couldn't believe what he had just read and wondered how the letter got there. Graeme wouldn't have been able to, and then a thought crossed his mind. He jumped up to get his phone but had forgotten about his shoulder; a surge of pain rushed through him and it brought tears to his eyes. He managed to grab his phone and hoped Natalie would answer unless she wasn't up yet.

The phone rang and rang but no answer, so it went straight to voicemail. He didn't want to leave a message, so he hung up and rang the number again. It took three or four times before eventually there was an answer.

"Hello," a husky female voice answered that had obviously just been woken up.

Grayson was now pacing backwards and forwards. "Natalie, is that you?"

Natalie coughed into the phone and nearly deafened Grayson but then replied, "Yeah, it's Natalie. Who's this?"

Now that he knew he was speaking to Natalie and not Lauren, he stopped pacing back and forth.

"I'm sorry I woke you, but this is very important."

Now Natalie was awake and she got out of bed quietly as Lauren was still sleeping. She could tell from the tone of Grayson's voice that something was wrong, so she went into another room to take the call. "What's wrong, Grayson?"

Grayson was now biting at his fingernails and replied, "Do me a favour and go to your front door and tell me, do you have a letter on the floor?" Natalie still half asleep, walked to the front door and to her astonishment there was a letter on the floor that had been slipped underneath. How would Grayson know this?

Natalie picked up the letter, looked at it and said, "Yeah, actually there is. How did you know? Did you put it there?"

Grayson put his head in his hand and replied, "No, I didn't put it there, but whatever you do, don't open it and for god's sake don't let Lauren see it." Now Natalie was confused and didn't understand why she wasn't supposed to open it if it was addressed to her.

She asked him, "Who's it from, Grayson and why shouldn't I open it?"

"Natalie the letter is from Graeme and you won't like what he has written, so the best thing you can do for both you and Lauren is to not read it and burn it. I read mine and he's trying to get in our heads. So please, just burn it."

She wanted to do what he said for Lauren's sake, but the cop in her really wanted to read it. Just then she realized something, and she was worried about the answer she was going to get but asked anyway. "Hold on a minute, Grayson. It can't be from Graeme as he's locked up, and he wouldn't have had the chance to put the letters under our doors, so how is it here?"

Just as she asked Grayson the question, a plausible answer came to her and she was dreading that he was going to verbally say what she was thinking. The thought sent shivers through her spine and just at that moment Lauren came out of the bedroom stretching, then rubbing her eyes. She saw Natalie on the phone and wondered who she was talking to.

Natalie saw Lauren out the corner of her eye and hid the letter so she wouldn't see it. She mouthed that she was on the phone with Grayson, and Lauren nodded then walked to the bathroom.

She turned her attention back to Grayson while looking at the letter, then Grayson replied to her question and she knew what he was going to say before she heard it. "Natalie, he has an accomplice"

The End (or is it?)